Portraits of a Mother

SHŪSAKU ENDŌ

Portraits of a Mother

A NOVELLA AND STORIES

Translated from the Japanese by Van C. Gessel

Foreword by Caryl Phillips

A MARGELLOS
WORLD REPUBLIC OF LETTERS BOOK

Yale UNIVERSITY PRESS | NEW HAVEN & LONDON

The Margellos World Republic of Letters is dedicated to making literary works from around the globe available in English through translation. It brings to the English-speaking world the work of leading poets, novelists, essayists, philosophers, and playwrights from Europe, Latin America, Africa, Asia, and the Middle East to stimulate international discourse and creative exchange.

Yale University Press books may be purchased in quantity for educational, business, or promotional use. For information, please e-mail sales.press@yale.edu (U.S. office) or sales@yaleup.co.uk (U.K. office).

Set in Source Serif type by Motto Publishing Services.
Printed in the United States of America.

ISBN 978-0-300-27943-6 (paperback : alk. paper)
Library of Congress Control Number: 2024942623
A catalogue record for this book is available from the British Library.

This paper meets the requirements of ANSI/NISO Z39.48-1992 (Permanence of Paper).

10 9 8 7 6 5 4 3 2 1

Foreword

By Caryl Phillips

In the spring of 2020, while organizing boxes of material belonging to the late writer Shūsaku Endō (1923–1996), a curator at the literary museum dedicated to his work in Nagasaki made the startling discovery of a previously unknown novella. This finding quickly became front-page news throughout Japan, and within a few months the novella appeared in print. Newly translated into English by the longstanding Endō scholar Van C. Gessel, the novella has been brought together with five stories—three of which were hitherto available only in Japanese—and is now being published here as *Portraits of a Mother: A Novella and Stories.*

One of the recently translated short stories, *A Six-Day Trip* (1968), concludes with a deeply affecting final paragraph in which we snatch a fleeting glimpse of a *father.*

> About a month after we returned to Tokyo, I was passing through Shibuya in a car. When I reached Kamitōri, a misty rain began to dampen my windshield, and fearing that my tires might slip, I slowed down and began a slow descent down the slope at Dōgenzaka. An elderly man wearing a fedora stood in the drizzling rain, searching in vain for a taxi. It was my father.

> Not once since I had broken off with him had I wanted to talk with him or even see his face, but during these five years he had lost a great deal of weight, and it looked as though his shoulders had stooped. For a brief moment, I felt nothing for him but pity. But I jammed my foot down on the accelerator to crush that feeling out of existence. My car glided past my father as he stood at the edge of the sidewalk, and for just an instant I had a close look at him in his fedora, but the image quickly vanished.

It is widely accepted that a great deal of the material that Endō utilizes for his fiction is thinly disguised autobiography. However, while Endō never shies away from introducing the problematic figure of the *mother* into his work, the *father* usually remains offstage. Intriguingly, in this story the father makes a surprising cameo appearance, albeit for the briefest of moments, which serves only to remind us of Endō's ambivalence with regard to the paternal presence. Endō's reluctance to place the father center stage, and perhaps give himself time to explore his ill will toward this perplexing character, is difficult to fathom, but this new collection helps us to better understand this mystery.

The two stories with which Endō's readers are already familiar—"Mothers" (1969), which appeared in *Stained Glass Elegies,* and "Shadows" (1968), which was published in *The Final Martyrs*—were both written shortly after the appearance of *Silence* (1966), the novel that is generally regarded as Endō's masterpiece. The disquieting themes that are touched upon in *Silence*—guilt, betrayal, and shame—are also present in these two stories, *and* in the three newly translated stories, which also date from the 1960s. In *Silence,* Endō's concerns are explored against the backdrop of a carefully constructed historical drama of early seventeenth-century Christian missionary zeal and apostasy, but in these five intimate stories we are able to witness the author engaging with guilt, betrayal, and shame by carefully tracing the turbulent emotional contours of his own life.

Shūsaku Endō was born in Tokyo in 1923, but he spent the early years of his childhood in Japanese-occupied Manchuria. His parents were ill-suited for each other, and by the time he was ten they had decided to separate. Endō returned with his mother to her hometown of Kobe, where he was raised by an aunt and baptized as a Catholic. At this time less than one percent of the Japanese population was Catholic, and Endō was bullied for his faith, which seems to have not only deepened his Christian beliefs, but also bestowed upon him a profound understanding of what it means to be an "outsider." After the Second World War, Endō was one of the first Japanese students to journey abroad. He traveled to France, where he studied Catholic literature at the University of Lyon, and this sojourn in Europe intensified his understanding of the existential difficulties of what it might mean to be "belong" with regard to nationality, religion, and—of course—family.

The evidence of his literary oeuvre suggests that it was painful for Endō to come to terms with his sense of alienation and abandonment regarding his mother, and he was unsure what to do with his antipathy toward his father. Every story in this new collection involves the narrator in the present time having his memory disturbed by something that causes him to cast his mind back to his unsettling upbringing. The prompt might be a research trip to an island, or a return to a former place of residence, or a tourist excursion to Israel, or an encounter in a Tokyo restaurant, or the perusal of an old photograph album. Whatever the stimulus, Endō creates a dramatic platform from which the flustered narrator feels compelled to step into his unstable past and ultimately punish himself by revisiting the guilt-ridden conundrum of why, and how, his elusive mother betrayed him—or perhaps it was he who betrayed her?

In the story "Mothers," the narrator's quest to find the *kakure* (hidden Christians) on a Japanese island and understand their shame at having apostasized many years before, slowly leads him to a consideration of his mother. The narrator is struck by the fact that, for the *kakure,*

> God was a stern paternal figure, and as a child asks its mother to intercede with its father, the *kakure* prayed for the Virgin Mary to intervene on their behalf.

The narrator then remembers that years earlier, a statue of the Virgin Mary, which his mother used to own, was damaged in an air raid during World War II. At night, he would often stare at what remained of the statue from his bed.

> It was unlike any Western painting or sculpture of the Mother of God that I had ever seen. . . . At some point I must have blended together the look on my mother's face and the expression on that statue.

There is a palpable yearning, on the part of the narrator, for the figure of the mother to somehow offer up salvation from the father, in much the same way that the *kakure* would pray to the Virgin Mary in the hope of soliciting her help.

In "Shadows," the other previously published story, a chance sighting of an old foreign priest in a Tokyo restaurant causes the narrator to feel that "Memories of my mother were spreading their roots deeply in my mind." The thoughts may relate to his mother but, against his will, the narrator finds himself drifting in the direction of the stern patriarch he has no desire to confront. He looks at the priest and quietly muses to himself, "I haven't yet written anything about my father, whom you never met . . . ," before forcing his mind to return to the subject of his mother.

The three newly translated stories are concerned with memories of a difficult mother who might swim into view at the slightest incitement, and thereafter plunge the narrator into a labyrinth of confusing, often contradictory, emotions. The mother always seems to expect too much, but she leaves before she is able to help the narrator along the path to fulfilling *her* wishes. Crucially, she is never able to fully protect him from the reductive gaze of the father whose appearances are, at best, momentary. It is only when we get to the profoundly unsettling novella, "Confronting the Shadows," that we finally achieve some fuller understanding of the role of the largely absent father in Endō's life and work.

In "Confronting the Shadows," the narrator sleeps next to his wife, and admits that there are "traits that he had inherited from his father and mother." The narrator then goes on to list the attributes that he believes he has inherited from his father and to characterize his subsequent relationship with him.

> His stooped posture, the cowardice and timidity that made him want to settle into a daily routine that would somehow

> enable him to just get by—those were traits he had likely inherited from his father. He despised the fact that he was prone to those tendencies, but mere disdain for his father was insufficient: he made every effort to fight back by hating his father at such times.

As the drama unfolds, the narrator's struggle to balance his conflicted feelings toward his mother with his unkind view of his father, and thereafter try to reach some conclusion as to what this *inheritance* has meant for him, becomes almost impossibly challenging. Surprisingly, in the end, there is both judgment *and* compassion in the portrait of his dejected father.

> He went out into what he thought was a deserted corridor, but his father was seated in a vacant chair facing the wall. A lonely shadow hovered over his father's back, as though no one would have anything to do with him. Staring at the lighted end of a cigarette that he wasn't smoking, his father could hear the sound of applause coming from the concert hall, but he showed no signs of moving from his spot.

Eventually, the narrator's parents divorce and, as we might have anticipated, the narrator suffers "because of his own weakness and cowardice in forsaking his mother." However, it is the occasionally tender focus on the father, beyond the demanding mother, that makes the story so compelling. We saw a quickly suppressed hint of sorrow for the father at the conclusion of "A Six-Day Trip," but here the father is not an eerie apparition at the side of a Tokyo street—he is center stage for the first and only time in Endō's work. Although the discord between father and son is clearly evident, there is some suggestion of empathy that, nevertheless, stops well short of forgiveness.

The novella was written in 1963, and it is therefore not juvenilia from the start of Endō's career, or a wistful late autumnal flourish. This is a writer working at the height of his powers. We cannot be sure why Endō chose not to publish "Confronting the Shadows" in his lifetime, but it is most likely because many of the people depicted in it were still alive and recognizable, and Endō probably decided to exercise discretion. In fact, in his Afterword to *The Final Martyrs,* Endō makes clear the connection between his fictional characters and his own life, and he is open about the way in which characters haunt him.

> Over the years I have forged intimate familial ties with [these] characters, who are reflections of a portion of myself. Consequently, even a character who appeared only once in a short story waits now in the wings, concealed by the curtain, for his next appearance on-stage. Not one of them has ever broken free of his familial ties with me and disappeared for ever—at least, not within the confines of my heart.

Although it is evident that the character of the mother never broke free of Endō, or he of her, "Confronting the Shadows" enables us to see the extent to which this was also true for the father. Across the years, in many works of fiction, Endō disparagingly describes the father as a somewhat cowardly man walking a safe asphalt road. Once again, toward the end of this newly discovered novella, we are asked to consider this same metaphor, only this time it is not the narrator who speaks, but the mother. As she does so, we not only glean insight into *her* character, and the life she has chosen, but we better understand the timid man she abandoned. In "Confronting the Shadows," Endō's father finally grows into visibility and becomes a real presence, albeit a predictably disappointing one when set against the dominant figure of the mother. After all, it is her quickening pulse, and clearly visible footprints, that will always constitute the heart of Endō's work.

> An asphalt-paved road is safe, so anyone can walk along it. There's no danger, so anybody can walk along it. But if a person on that path turns and looks behind them, not a single one of their footsteps has been left on that safe road. A sandy beach by the ocean is difficult to walk along. It's a difficult path, but when you look behind you, every single one of your footsteps remains there. That's the kind of life your mother has chosen.

His mother's decision to choose this "kind of life" haunted Endō, and these elegant, yet often anxiety-wracked, stories enable us to gain some perspective on the parental angst that underpinned so much of Endō's writing.

Portraits of a Mother

Mothers

I reached the dock at nightfall.

The ferry boat had not yet arrived. I peered over the low wall of the quay. Small gray waves laden with refuse and leaves licked at the jetty like a puppy quietly lapping up water. A single truck was parked in the vacant lot by the dock; beyond the lot stood two warehouses. A man had lit a bonfire in front of one of the warehouses; the red flames flickered.

In the waiting room, five or six local men wearing high boots sat patiently on benches, waiting for the ticket booth to open. At their feet were dilapidated trunks and boxes loaded with fish. I also noticed several cages packed full of chickens. The birds thrust their long necks through the wire mesh and writhed as though in pain. The men sat quietly on the benches, occasionally glancing in my direction.

I felt as though I had witnessed a scene like this in some Western painting. But I couldn't recall who had sketched it, or when I had seen it.

The lights on the broad gray shore of the island across the water twinkled faintly. Somewhere a dog was howling, but I couldn't tell whether it was over on the island or here on my side of the bay.

Gradually some of the lights that I had thought belonged

to the island began to move. I finally realized that they belonged to the ferry boat that was heading this way. At last the ticket booth opened, and the men got up from the benches and formed a queue. When I lined up behind them, the smell of fish was overpowering. I had heard that most of the people on the island mixed farming with fishing.

Their faces all looked the same. Their eyes seemed sunken, perhaps because of the protruding cheekbones; their faces were void of expression, as if they were afraid of something. In short, dishonesty and dread had joined together to mold the faces of these islanders. Perhaps I felt that way because of the preconceived notions I had about the island I was about to visit. Throughout the Edo period, the residents of the island had suffered through poverty, hard, grinding labor, and religious persecution.

After some time I boarded the ferry boat, which soon pulled away from the harbor. Only three trips a day connected the island with the Kyushu mainland. Until just two years before, boats had made the crossing only twice a day, once in the morning and once in the evening.

It was in fact little more than a large motor launch and had no seats. The passengers stood between bicycles and fish crates and old trunks, exposed to the chilling sea winds that blew through the windows. Had this been Tokyo, some passengers would undoubtedly have complained at the conditions, but here no one said a word. The only sound was the grinding of the boat's engine; even the chickens in the cages at our feet did not utter a peep. I jabbed at some of the chickens with the tip of my shoe. A look of fear darted across their faces. They looked just like the men from the waiting room, and I had to smile.

The wind whipped up; the sea was dark, and the waves black. I tried several times to light a cigarette, but the wind extinguished my match at every attempt. The unlit cigarette grew damp from my lips, and finally I hurled it overboard . . . though the winds may very well have blown it back onto the boat. The weariness of the twelve-hour bus ride from Nagasaki overcame me. I was stiff from the small of my back to my shoulders. I closed my eyes and listened to the droning of the engine.

Several times, out on the pitch-black ocean, the pounding of the engine grew suddenly faint. In an instant it would surge up again, only to slacken once more. I listened to that process repeat itself several times before I opened my eyes again. The lights of the island were directly ahead.

"Hello!" a voice called. "Is Watanabe there? Throw the line!"

There was a dull, heavy thud as the line was thrown to the quay.

I got off after the locals had disembarked. The cold night wind bore the smells of fish and the sea. Just beyond the dock gate stood five or six shops selling dried fish and local souvenirs. I had heard that the best-known local product was a dried flying fish called *ago.* A man dressed in boots and wearing a jacket stood in front of the shops. He watched me closely as I stepped through the gate, then came up to me and said, "Sensei, thank you for coming all this way. The church sent me to meet you."

He bowed to me an embarrassing number of times, then tried to wrest my suitcase from my hands. No matter how often I refused, he would not let go of it. The palms that brushed against my hand were as solid and large as the root of a tree. They were not like the soft, damp hands of the Tokyo Christians that I knew so well.

I tried to walk beside him, but he stubbornly maintained a distance of one pace behind me. I remembered that he had called me "Sensei," and I felt bewildered. If the church people persisted in addressing me in terms of respect, the locals might be put on their guard against me.

The smell of fish that permeated the harbor trailed persistently after us. That odor seemed to have embedded itself in the low-roofed houses and the narrow road over the course of many years. Off to my left, across the sea, the lights of Kyushu now shone faintly in the darkness.

"How is the Father?" I asked. "I came as soon as I got his letter . . ."

But there was no answer from behind. I tried to detect whether I had done something to offend him, but that did not appear to be the case. Perhaps he was just diffident and determined not to engage in idle chatter. Or possibly, after long years of experience, the people of this island had concluded that the best way to protect themselves was to avoid imprudent conversation.

I had met their priest in Tokyo. He had come up from Kyushu to attend a meeting just after I had published a novel about the Christian era in Japan. I went up and introduced myself to him. He too had the deep-set eyes and prominent cheekbones of the island's fishermen. Bewildered perhaps to be in Tokyo among all the notable clerics and nuns, his face tightened and he said very little when I spoke to him. In that sense, he was very much like the man who was now carrying my suitcase.

"Do you know Father Fukabori?" I had asked the priest.

A year earlier, I had taken a bus to a fishing village an hour from Nagasaki. There I met the village priest, Father Fukabori, who was from the Urakami district. Not only did he teach me how to deep-sea fish, he also provided me with considerable assistance in my research. The purpose of my visit had been to visit the *kakure,* descendants of some of the original Christian converts in the seventeenth century who had, over the span of many years, gradually corrupted the religious practices. Father Fukabori took me to the homes of several of the *kakure,* who still stubbornly refused to be reconverted to Catholicism. As I have said, the faith of the *kakure* Christians over the long years of national isolation had drifted far from true Christianity and had embraced elements of Shinto, Buddhism, and local superstition. Because of this, one of the missions of the Church in this region, ever since the arrival of Father Petitjean in the Meiji period, was the reconversion of the *kakure* who were scattered throughout the Gotō and Ikitsuki Islands.

"He let me stay at his church." I continued to grasp for threads of conversation, but the priest clutched his glass of juice tightly and muttered only monosyllabic responses.

"Are there any *kakure* in your parish?"

"Yes."

"They're starting to show up on television these days, and they look a little happier now that they're making some money out of it. The old man that Father Fukabori introduced me to was just like an announcer on a variety show. Is it easy to meet the *kakure* on your island?"

"No, it's very difficult."

Our conversation broke off there, and I moved on in search of more congenial company.

Yet, to my surprise, a month ago I received a letter from this artless country priest. It opened with the customary Catholic "Peace of the Lord" salutation and went on to say that he had persuaded some of the *kakure* who lived in his parish to show me their religious icons and copies of their prayers. His handwriting was surprisingly fluent.

I looked back at the man walking behind me and asked, "Are there any *kakure* around here?"

He shook his head. "No, they all live in the mountains."

Half an hour later we reached the church. A man dressed in a black cassock, his hands clasped behind him, stood at the doorway. Beside him was a young man with a bicycle.

Since I had already met the priest—though only once—I greeted him casually, but he looked somewhat perplexed and glanced at the other two men. I had been thoughtless. I had forgotten that, unlike in Tokyo or Osaka, in this district the priest was like a village headman, or in some cases as highly respected as a feudal lord.

"Jirō, go and tell Mr. Nakamura that the Sensei has arrived," he ordered. With a deep bow the young man climbed on his bicycle and disappeared into the darkness.

"Which way is the *kakure* village?" I asked. The priest pointed in the opposite direction to that from which I had come. I couldn't see any lights, perhaps because the mountains obstructed my view. In the age of persecution, to escape the eyes of the officials, the *kakure* Christians had settled as much as possible in secluded mountain fastnesses or on inaccessible coastlines. Undoubtedly that was the case here. We'll have to walk quite a way tomorrow, I thought, surveying my own rather fragile body. Seven years before, I had undergone chest surgery, and though I had recovered, I still had little faith in my physical strength.

* * *

I dreamed of my mother. In my dream I had just been brought out of the operating theater, and was sprawled out on my bed like a corpse. A rubber tube connected to an oxygen tank was thrust into my nostril, and intravenous needles pierced my right arm and leg, carrying blood from the transfusion bottles dangling over my bed.

Although I should have been half unconscious, through the languid weight of the anesthetic I recognized the gray shadow that held my hand. It was my mother. Strangely, neither my wife nor any of the doctors were in the room.

I have had that dream many times. Frequently I wake up unable to distinguish dream from reality and lie in a daze on my bed, until I realize with a sigh that I am not in the hospital where I spent three years, but in my own home.

I have not told my wife about that dream. She was the one who watched over me through every night after each of my three operations, and I felt remorseful that my wife did not even seem to exist in my dreams. The main reason I said nothing to her, however, was my distasteful realization that the firm bonds between my mother and myself—stronger than even I had suspected—continued to link us some twenty years after her death, even in my dreams.

I know little about psychoanalysis, so I have no idea exactly what this dream means. In it, I cannot actually see my mother's face. Nor are her movements distinct. When I reflect back on the dream, the figure seems to be my mother, but I cannot positively say that it is. But it most definitely is not my wife or any kind of nurse or attendant, or even a doctor.

So far as my memory serves me, I can recollect no experience in my youth when I lay ill in bed with my mother holding my hand. Normally the image of my mother that pops into my mind is the figure of a woman who lived her life fervently.

When I was five years old, we were living in Dalian in Manchuria in connection with my father's work. I can still vividly recall the icicles that hung down past the windows of our tiny house like the teeth of a fish. The sky is overcast, and it looks as if it will begin to snow at any moment, but the snow never comes. In a nine-by-twelve room my mother is practicing the violin. For hours on end she practices the same melody over and over again. With the violin wedged under her chin, her face is hard, stone-like, and her eyes are fixed on a single point in space as she seems to be trying to isolate that one true note somewhere in the void. Unable to find that elusive note, she heaves a sigh; her irritation mounts, and she continues to scrape the bow across the strings. The brownish calluses on her chin were familiar to me. They had formed when she was still a student at the music academy and had kept her violin tucked constantly under her chin. The tips of her fingers, too, were as hard to the touch as pebbles, the result of the many thousands of times she had pressed down on the strings in her quest for that one note.

The image of my mother in my school days—that image within my heart was of a woman abandoned by her husband. She sits like a stone statue on the sofa in the dark room at nightfall in Dalian. As a child I could not bear to see her struggling so to endure her grief. I sat near her, pretending to do my homework but concentrating every nerve in my body on her. Because I could not fathom the complex situation, I was all the more affected by the picture of her suffering, her hand pressed against her forehead. I was in torment, not knowing what I should do.

Those dismal days stretched from autumn into winter. Determined not to see her sitting in that darkened room, I walked home from school as slowly as I could. I followed the old White Russian who sold Russian bread everywhere he went. Around sunset I finally turned toward home, kicking pebbles along the side of the road.

One day, when my father had taken me out on one of our rare walks together, he said suddenly, "Your mother . . . she's going back to Japan on an important errand . . . Would you like to go with her?"

Detecting a grown-up's lie, I grunted, "Un-huh," and went on walking along behind him in silence, kicking at every rock I could find. The following month, with financial assistance from her older sister in Kobe, my mother took me back to Japan.

And then my mother during my middle-school days. Though I have various memories of her, they all congeal on one spot. Just as she had once played her violin in search of the one true note, she subsequently adopted a stern, solitary life in quest of the one true religion. On wintry mornings, at the frozen fissure of dawn, I often noticed a light in her room. I knew what she was doing in there. She was fingering the beads of her rosary and praying. Eventually she would take me with her on the first Hankyū-line train of the day and set out for Mass. On the deserted train I slouched back in my seat and pretended to be rowing a boat. But occasionally I would open my eyes and see my mother's fingers gliding along those rosary beads.

* * *

In the darkness, I opened my eyes to the sound of rain. I dressed hurriedly and ran from my bungalow to the brick chapel across the way.

The chapel was almost too ornate for this beggarly island village. The previous evening, the priest had told me that the village Christians had worked for two years to erect this chapel, hauling the stones and cutting the wood themselves. They say that three hundred years ago, the faithful also built churches with their own hands to please the foreign missionaries. That custom has been passed down undiluted on this remote island off Kyushu.

In the dimly lit chapel knelt three peasant women in their work attire, with white cloths covering their heads. There were also two men in working clothes. Since the nave was bereft of kneelers or benches, they each knelt on straw mats to offer up their prayers. One had the impression that, as soon as Mass was over, they would pick up their hoes and head straight for the fields or the sea. At the altar, the priest turned his sunken eyes toward the tiny congregation, lifted up the chalice with both hands, and intoned the prayer for Consecration. The light from the candles illuminated the text of the large Latin missal. I thought of my mother. I couldn't help but feel that this chapel somehow resembled the church she and I had attended thirty years before.

When we stepped outside after Mass the rain had stopped,

but a dense fog had settled in. The direction in which the *kakure* village lay was shrouded in a milky haze; the silhouettes of trees hovered like ghosts amid the fog.

"It doesn't look like you'll be able to set out in all this fog," the priest muttered from behind me, rubbing his hands together. "The mountain roads are very slippery. You'd better spend the day resting yourself. Why don't you go tomorrow?"

He proposed a tour of the Christian graves in his village for the afternoon. Since the *kakure* district lay deep in the mountains, it would be no easy matter for even a local resident to make the climb, and with only one lung I certainly did not have the strength to walk there in the dense, soaking mist.

Through breaks in the fog, the ocean appeared, black and cold. Not a single boat had ventured out. Even from where I stood, I could make out the frothy white fangs of the waves.

I had breakfast with the priest and went to lie down in the six-mat room that had been provided for me. In bed I reread a book about the history of this region. A thin rain began to fall; its sound, like shifting sands, deepened the solitude within my room, which was bare except for a bus timetable tacked to the wall. Suddenly I wanted to go back to Tokyo.

According to the historical documents, the persecution of Christians in this area commenced in 1607 and was at its fiercest between 1615 and 1617.

Father Pedro de San Dominico
Matthias
Francisco Gorosuke
Miguel Shin'emon
Dominico Kisuke

This list includes only the names of the priests and monks who were martyred in the village in 1615. No doubt there were many more nameless peasants and fisherwomen who gave up their lives for the faith. In the past, as I devoted my free time to reading the history of Christian martyrdoms in Japan, I formulated in my mind an audacious theory. My hypothesis is that these public executions might have been carried out as warnings to the leaders of each village rather than to each individual believer. This will, of course, never be anything more than my own private conjecture so long as the historical records offer no supportive evidence. But I can't help feeling that the faithful in those days, rather than deciding individually whether to die for the faith or to apostatize, were instead bowing to the will of the entire community.

It has been my long-held supposition that, because the sense of community, based on blood relationships, was so much stronger among villagers in those days, it was not left up to individuals to determine whether they would endure persecution or succumb. Instead this matter was decided by the village as a whole. In other words, the officials, knowing that they would be exterminating their labor force if they executed an entire community that stubbornly clung to its faith, would only kill selected representatives of the village. In cases where there was no choice but apostasy, the villagers would renounce their beliefs en masse to ensure the preservation of the community. That, I felt, was the fundamental distinction between Japanese Christian martyrdoms and the martyrs in foreign lands.

The historical documents clearly indicate that in former times, nearly fifteen hundred Christians lived on this ten-by-three-and-a-half-kilometer island. The most active proselytizer on the island in those days was the Portuguese father Camillo Constanzo, who was burned at the stake on the beach of Tabira in 1622. They say that even after the fire was lit and his body was engulfed in black smoke, the crowd could hear him singing the *Laudate Dominum*. When he finished singing, he cried "Holy! Holy!" five times and breathed his last.

Peasants and fishermen found to be practicing Christianity were executed on a craggy islet—appropriately named the Isle of Rocks—about a half hour from here by rowing boat. They were bound hand and foot, taken to the top of the sheer precipice of the island, and hurled to their deaths. At the height of the persecutions, the number of believers killed on the Isle of Rocks never fell below ten per month, according to contemporary reports. To simplify matters, the officers would sometimes bind several prisoners together in a rush mat and toss them into the frigid seas. Virtually none of the bodies of these martyrs were ever recovered.

I read over the grisly history of the island's martyrs until past noon. The drizzling rain continued to fall.

At lunchtime the priest was nowhere to be seen. A sunburned middle-aged woman with jutting cheekbones served my meal. I judged her to be the wife of some fisherman, but in the course of conversation I learned to my surprise that she was a nun who had devoted herself to a life of celibate service. The image I had always fostered of nuns was limited to those women I often saw in Tokyo with their peculiar black robes. This woman told me about the order of sisters in this area, known in the local jargon as "The Servants' Quarters." The order, to which she belonged, practiced communal living, worked in the fields the same as the other farm women, looked after children at the nursery school, and tended the sick in the hospital.

"Father went on his motorcycle to Mount Fudō. He said he'd be back around three o'clock." Her eyes shifted toward the rain-splattered window. "With this awful weather, you must be terribly bored, Sensei. Jirō from the office said he'd be by soon to show you the Christian graves."

Jirō was the young man with the bicycle who had been standing beside the priest when I arrived the previous night.

Just as she predicted, Jirō appeared soon after I had finished lunch and invited me to accompany him. He even brought along a pair of boots for me to wear.

"I didn't think you'd want to get your shoes all muddy."

He apologized that the boots were so old, bowing his head so incessantly that I was embarrassed.

"I'm ashamed to make you ride in a truck like this," he added.

As we drove along the streets in his little van, I found that the mental picture I had drawn the previous night was accurate. All the houses were squat, and the village reeked of fish. At the dock, about ten small boats were preparing to go to sea. The only buildings made of reinforced concrete were the village office and the primary school. Even the "main street" gave way to thatched-roofed farmhouses after less than five minutes. The telephone poles were plastered with rain-soaked advertisements for a strip show. They featured a picture of a nude woman cupping her breasts; the show bore the dreadful title "The Sovereign of Sex."

"Father is heading a campaign to stop these shows in the village."

"But I'll bet the young men spend all their free time there. Even the young Christians . . ."

My attempt at humor fell on deaf ears as Jirō tightened his grip on the steering wheel. I quickly changed the subject.

"About how many Christians are there on the island now?"

"I think around a thousand."

In the seventeenth century the number had been calculated at fifteen hundred, meaning a loss of about one-third since that time.

"And how many *kakure*?"

"I'm really not sure. I imagine they get fewer in number every year. Only the old people stick to their practices. The young ones say the whole thing's ridiculous."

Jirō related an interesting story. In spite of frequent encouragement from the priests and believers, the *kakure* had refused to reconvert to Catholicism. They claimed that it was their brand of Christianity that had been handed down from their ancestors, making it the true original faith; they further insisted that the Catholicism brought back to Japan in the Meiji period was a reformed religion. Their suspicions were confirmed by the modem attire of the priests, which differed radically from that of the padres they had been told about over the generations.

"And so one French priest had a brilliant idea. He dressed up like one of the padres from those days and went to visit the *kakure*."

"What happened?"

"The *kakure* admitted he looked a lot like the real thing, but something was wrong. They just couldn't believe him!"

I sensed a degree of contempt toward the *kakure* in Jirō's

tale, but I laughed aloud anyway. Surely the French priest who went to all the trouble of dressing up like a friar from the seventeenth century had had a sense of humor about him. The story seemed somehow exhilaratingly typical of this island.

Once we left the village, the gray road extended out along the coast. Mountains pressed in from our left, the ocean to our right. The waters churned, a leaden color, and when I rolled down the window an inch, a gust of rainy wind pelted my face.

Jirō stopped his truck in the shelter of a windbreak and held out an umbrella for me. The earth was sandy, dotted here and there with growths of tiny pine shrubs. The Christian graveyard lay at the crest of a sand dune perched precariously over the ocean. It hardly deserved to be called a graveyard. The single stone marker was so tiny that even I could have lifted it with a little effort, and a good third of it was buried beneath the sand. The face of the stone was bleached gray by the wind and rain; all that I could make out was a cross that seemed to have been scratched into the rock with some object, and the Roman letters M and R. Those two characters suggested a name like "Maria," and I wondered if the Christian buried here might have been a woman.

I had no idea why this solitary grave had been dug in a spot so far removed from the village. Perhaps some relative had quietly moved it to this inconspicuous location after the exterminations. Or possibly, during the persecution, this woman had been executed on this very beach.

A choppy sea stretched out beyond this forsaken Christian grave. The gusts pounding the windbreak sounded like electric wires chafing together. In the offing I could see a tiny black island, the Isle of Rocks where Christians from this district had been strung together like beads and hurled into the waters below.

* * *

I learned how to lie to my mother.

As I think back on it now, I suppose my lies must have sprung from some sort of complex I had about her. This woman, who had been driven to seek consolation in religion after being abandoned by her husband, had redirected the fervor she had once expended in search of the one true violin note toward a quest for the one true God. I can comprehend that zeal now, but as a child it suffocated me. The more she compelled me to share her faith, the more I fought her oppressive power, the way a drowning child struggles against the pressure of the water.

One of my friends at school was a boy called Tamura. His father ran a brothel at Nishinomiya. He always had a filthy bandage wound about his neck and he was often absent from school; I suppose he must have had tuberculosis even then. He had very few friends and was constantly mocked by the conscientious students. Certainly part of the reason I latched on to him was a desire to get back at my strict mother.

The first time I smoked a cigarette under Tamura's tutelage, I felt as though I was committing a horrid sin. Behind the archery range at school, Tamura, sensitive to every noise around us, stealthily pulled a crumpled cigarette pack from the pocket of his school uniform.

"You can't inhale deeply right at first. Try just a little puff at a time."

I hacked, choked by the piercing smoke that filled my nose and throat. At that moment, my mother's face appeared before me. It was her face as she prayed with her rosary in the predawn darkness. I took a deeper drag on the cigarette to exorcize this vision.

Another thing I learned from Tamura was going to movies on my way home from school. I slipped into the darkened Niban Theater near the Nishinomiya Hanshin Station, following Tamura like a criminal. The smell from the toilet filled the auditorium. Amid the sounds of crying babies and the coughs of old men, I listened to the monotonous gyrations of the movie projector. My whole mind was absorbed with thoughts of what my mother would be doing just then.

"Let's go home."

Over and over I pressed Tamura to leave, until finally he snarled angrily, "Stop pestering me! Go home by yourself, then!"

When we finally went outside, the Hanshin train that sped past us was carrying workers back to their homes.

"You've got to stop being so scared of your mother." Tamura shrugged his shoulders derisively. "Just make up a good excuse."

After we parted, I walked along the deserted road, trying to think up a convincing lie. I hadn't come up with one until I stepped through the doorway.

"We had some extra classes today," I caught my breath and blurted out. "They said we have to start preparing for entrance exams." When it was obvious that my mother had believed me, a pain clutched at my chest even as I experienced an inner feeling of satisfaction.

To be quite honest, I had no true religious faith whatsoever. Although I attended church at my mother's insistence, I merely cupped my hands together and made as if to pray, while inwardly my mind roamed over empty landscapes. I recalled scenes from the many movies I had seen with Tamura, and I even thought about the photographs of naked women he had shown me one day. Inside the chapel the faithful stood or knelt in response to the prayers of the priest reciting the Mass. The more I tried to restrain my fantasies, the more they flooded into my brain with mocking clarity.

I truly could not understand why my mother believed in such a religion. The words of the priest, the stories in the Bible, the crucifix—they all seemed like intangible happenings from a past that had nothing to do with us. I doubted the sincerity of the people who gathered there each Sunday to clasp their hands in prayer even as they scolded their children and cleared their throats. Sometimes I would regret such thoughts and feel apologetic toward my mother. And I prayed that, if there was a God, He would grant me a believing heart. But there was no reason to think that such a plea would change how I felt.

Finally I stopped going to morning Mass altogether. My excuse was that I had to study for my entrance exams. I felt not the slightest qualms when, after that, I lay in bed listening to my mother's footsteps as she set out alone for church each winter morning. By then she had already begun to complain of heart spasms. Eventually I stopped going to church even on Sundays, though out of consideration for my mother's feelings I left the house and then slipped away to pass my time wandering around the bustling shopping center at Nishinomiya or staring at the advertisements in front of the movie theaters.

Around that time Mother often had trouble breathing.

Sometimes, just walking down the street, she would stop suddenly and clutch her chest, her face twisted into an ugly grimace. I ignored her. A sixteen-year-old boy could not imagine what it was to fear death. The attacks passed quickly, and she was back to normal within five minutes, so I assumed it was nothing serious. In reality, her many years of torment and weariness had worn out her heart. Even so, she still got up at five o'clock every morning and, dragging her heavy legs, walked to the station down the deserted road. The church was two stops away on the train.

One Saturday, unable to resist the temptation, I decided to play truant from school and got off the train near an amusement district. I left my school bag at a coffee shop that Tamura and I had begun to frequent. I still had quite a bit of time before the film started. In my pocket I carried a one-yen note I had taken from my mother's purse several days earlier. Somewhere along the way I had picked up the habit of dipping into her wallet. I sat through several movies until sunset, then returned home with a look of innocence on my face.

When I opened the door, I was surprised to see my mother standing there. She stared at me without saying a word. Then slowly her face contorted, and tears trickled down her twisted cheeks. It seems she had found out everything through a phone call from my school. She wept softly in the room adjoining mine until late into the night. I stuck my fingers in my ears, trying to block out the sound, but somehow it insinuated itself into my eardrums. Thoughts of a convenient lie to get me out of this situation left me little room for remorse.

* * *

Afterward Jirō took me to the village office. While I was examining some local artifacts, sunlight began to warm the windows. I glanced up and saw that the rain had finally stopped.

"You can see a few more of these if you go over to the school." Mr. Nakamura, a deputy official in the village, stood beside me with a worried expression on his face, as though it were his personal responsibility that there was nothing here worth looking at. The only displays at the village office and the elementary school were of some earthenware fragments from remote antiquity, dug up by the teachers at the school. They had none of the *kakure* relics that I was eager to examine.

"Don't you have any *kakure* rosaries or crosses?"

Mr. Nakamura shook his head with embarrassed regret. "Those people like to keep things to themselves. You'll just have to go there yourself. They're a bunch of eccentrics, if you ask me."

His words were filled with the same contempt for the *kakure* that I had detected in Jirō's remarks.

Jirō, having observed the weather conditions, returned to the village office and announced cheerfully, "It's cleared up. We'll be able to go tomorrow for sure. Would you like to go and see the Isle of Rocks now?"

When we had visited the Christian grave, I had especially asked to see the Isle of Rocks.

Mr. Nakamura made a quick phone call to the fishermen's union. Village offices can be useful at such times; the union was more than willing to provide us with a small motorboat.

I borrowed a mackintosh from Mr. Nakamura. He accompanied Jirō and me to the dock, where a fisherman had the boat waiting. A mat had been laid in the wet bilges for us to sit on. In the murky waters that slopped around our feet floated the tiny silver body of a dead fish.

With a buzz from the motor, the boat set out into the still rough seas, vibrating ever more fiercely. It was invigorating to ride the crest of a wave, but each time we sank into a trough, I felt as though my stomach were cramping.

"The fishing's good at the Isle of Rocks," Nakamura commented. "We often go there on holidays. Do you fish, Sensei?"

When I shook my head, he gave me a disappointed look and began boasting to Jirō and the fisherman about the large silthead he had once caught.

The spray drenched my mackintosh. The chill of the sea winds rendered me speechless. The surface of the water, which had started out gray, was now a dark, cold-looking black. I thought of the Christians who had been hurled into these waters four centuries before. If I had been born in such a time, I would not have had the strength to endure such a punishment. Suddenly I thought of my mother. I saw myself strolling around the entertainment district at Nishinomiya, then telling lies to my mother.

The little island drew closer. True to its name, it was composed entirely of craggy rocks, the very crest of which was crowned with a scant growth of vegetation. In response to a question from me, Mr. Nakamura reported that, aside from occasional visits by officials of the Ministry of Postal Services, the island was used by the villagers only as a place from which to fish.

Ten or so crows squawked hoarsely as they hovered over the top of the islet. Their calls pierced the wet gray sky, giving the scene an eerie, desolate air. Now we had a clear view of the cracks and fissures in the rocks. The waves beat against the crags with a roar, spewing up white spray.

I asked to see the spot from which the Christians were

cast into the sea, but neither Jirō nor Nakamura knew where it was. Most likely there had not been one particular location; the faithful had probably been thrown down from any convenient place.

"It's frightening even to think about it."

"It's impossible to imagine nowadays."

Evidently the thoughts that had been running through my head had not even occurred to my two Catholic companions.

"There's lots of bats in these caves. When you get up close, you can hear them shrieking."

"They're strange creatures. They fly so fast, and yet they never bump into anything. I hear they've got something like radar."

"Well, Sensei, shall we take a walk around and then go back?"

The island from which we had come was being pounded by white surf. The rainclouds split open, and we had a clear view of the mountain slopes in the distance.

Mr. Nakamura, pointing toward the mountains as the priest had done the previous evening, said, "That's where the *kakure* village is."

"Nowadays I suppose they don't keep to themselves like they used to, do they?"

"As a matter of fact, they do. We had one working as a janitor at the school. Shimomura was his name. He was from the *kakure* village. But I didn't much care for him. There wasn't anything to talk to him about."

The two men explained that the Catholics on the island were hesitant about associating with the *kakure* or intermarrying with them. Their reluctance seemed to have more to do with psychological conflicts than with religious differences. Even now the *kakure* married their own kind; if they did otherwise, they would not be able to preserve their faith. This custom reinforced their conviction that they were a peculiar people.

On the breast of those mountains half concealed in mist, the *kakure* Christians had sustained their religious faith for three hundred years, guarding their secret institutions from outsiders, as was done in all the *kakure* villages, by appointing people to such special village posts as "Waterworks Official," "Watchman," "Greeter," and "Ombudsman." From grandfather to father, and from father to son, their formal prayers were passed through the generations, and their objects of worship were concealed behind the dark Buddhist altars. My eyes searched the mountain slope for that isolated village, as though I were gazing at some forsaken landscape. But of course it was impossible to spot it from there.

"Sensei, why are you interested in such a strange group of people?" Nakamura asked me in amazement. My reply was noncommittal.

* * *

One clear autumn day, I bought some chrysanthemums and set out for the cemetery. My mother's grave is in a Catholic cemetery in Fuchū. I can't begin to count the number of times I have made the journey to that graveyard since my school days. In the past, the road was surrounded by groves of chestnut and buckeye trees and fields of wheat; in the spring it was a pleasant path for a leisurely stroll. But now it is a busy thoroughfare crowded with all manner of shops. Even the stone carver's little hut that once stood all by itself at the entrance to the cemetery has turned into a solid one-story building.

Memories flood my mind each time I visit that place. I went to pay my respects the day I graduated from the university. The day before I was due to board a ship for France to continue my studies, I again made the journey there. It was the first spot I visited when I fell ill and had to return to Japan. I was careful to visit the grave on the day I was married, and on the day I went into the hospital. Sometimes I make the pilgrimage without telling anyone, not even my wife. It is the spot where I conduct private conversations with my mother. In the depths of my heart lurks a desire not to be disturbed even by those who are close to me. I make my way down the path. A statue of the Holy Mother stands in the center of the graveyard, surrounded by a tidy row of stone markers belonging to the graves of foreign nuns who have been buried here in Japan. Branching out from this center point are white crosses and gravestones. A bright sun and a peaceful silence hover over each of the graves.

Mother's grave is small. My heart constricts whenever I look at that tiny grave marker. I pluck the wild grasses that surround it. With buzzing wings, insects swarm around me as I work in solitude. There is no other sound.

As I pour a ladle of water into the flower vase, I think (as I always do) of the day my mother died. The memory is a painful one for me. I was not with her when she collapsed in the hallway from a heart attack, nor was I beside her when she died. I was at Tamura's house, doing something that would have made her weep had she seen it.

Tamura had pulled a sheaf of postcards wrapped in newspaper from his desk drawer. And he smiled that thin smile he always wore when he was about to teach me something.

"These aren't like the phony ones they sell around here."

There were something like ten photographs inside the

newspaper wrapping. Their edges were yellow and faded. The dark figure of a man was stretched out on top of the white body of a woman. She had a look as though of pain on her face. I caught my breath and flipped through the pictures one after another.

"Lecher! You've seen enough, haven't you?" Tamura cackled.

Their telephone rang, and after it was answered, we heard footsteps approaching. Hurriedly Tamura stuffed the photographs into his drawer. A woman's voice called my name.

"You must go home right away! Your mother's had an attack!"

"What's up?" Tamura asked.

"I don't know." I was still glancing at the drawer. "How did she know I was here?"

I was less concerned about her attack than the fact that she knew I was at Tamura's. She had forbidden me to go there after she found out that Tamura's father ran a whorehouse. It was not unusual for her to have to go to bed with heart palpitations, but if she took the white pills (I've forgotten the name) that the doctor gave her, the attack was always brought under control.

I made my way slowly along the back streets still warmed by the bright sun. Rusted scraps of metal were piled up in a field, marked with a "For Sale" sign. Beside the field was a small factory. I didn't know what they manufactured there, but a dull, heavy, pounding noise was repeated regularly inside the building. A man came riding toward me on a bicycle, but he stopped beside the dusty, weed-covered field and began to urinate.

My house came into view. The window to my room was

half open, the way it always was. Neighborhood children were playing in front of the house. Everything was normal, and there was no sign that anything unusual had happened. The priest from our church was standing at the front door.

"Your mother . . . died just a few moments ago." He spoke each word softly and clearly. Even a mindless middle-school student like myself could tell that he was struggling to suppress the emotion in his voice. Even a mindless middle-school student like myself could sense the criticism in his voice.

In the back room, my mother's body was surrounded by neighbors and people from the church, sitting with stooped shoulders. No one turned to look at me; no one spoke a word to me. I knew from the stiffness of their backs that they all were condemning me.

Mother's face was white as milk. A shadow of pain still lingered between her brows. Her expression reminded me of the look on the face of the woman in the photographs I had just been examining. Only then did I realize what I had done, and I wept.

I finish pouring the water from the bucket and put the chrysanthemums into the vase that is part of the gravestone. The insects that have been buzzing about my face now cluster around the flowers. The earth beneath which my mother lies is the dark soil peculiar to the Musashi Plain. At some point I too will be buried here, and as in my youth, I will be living alone again with my mother.

* * *

I had not given Mr. Nakamura a satisfactory answer when he asked me why I was interested in the *kakure.*

Public curiosity about the *kakure* has increased recently. This "hidden" religion is an ideal subject for investigation by those doing research in comparative religion. NHK, the national educational channel, has done several features on the *kakure* of Gotō and Ikitsuki, and many of the foreign priests of my acquaintance come to visit the *kakure* whenever they are in Nagasaki. But I am interested in the *kakure* for only one reason—because they are the offspring of apostates. Like their ancestors, they cannot utterly abandon their faith; instead they live out their lives, consumed by remorse and dark guilt and shame.

I was first drawn to these descendants of apostates after I had written a novel set in the Christian era. Sometimes I catch a glimpse of myself in these *kakure,* people who have had to lead lives of duplicity, lying to the world and never revealing their true feelings to anyone. I too have a secret that I have never told anyone, and that I will carry within myself until the day I die.

That evening I drank *sake* with the Father, Jirō, and Mr. Nakamura. The nun who had served me lunch brought out a large tray stacked with raw sea urchins and abalone. The local *sake* was too sweet for someone like myself who drinks only the dry variety, but the sea urchins were so fresh they made the Nagasaki ones seem almost stale. The rain had let up earlier, but it began to pour again. Jirō got drunk and began to sing.

> Oh, let us go, let us go
> To the Temple of Paradise, let us go,
> Oh, oh.
> They call it the Temple of Paradise,

They say it is spacious and grand.
But whether it is large or small
Is really up to my heart.

I knew the song. When I'd visited Hirado two years before, the Christians there had taught it to me. The melody was complicated and impossible to remember, but as I listened to Jirō's plaintive singing, I thought of the dark expressions on the faces of the *kakure*. Protruding cheekbones and sunken eyes that seemed to be fixed on a single point in space. Perhaps, as they waited through the long years of national isolation for the boats of the missionaries that might never return, they muttered this song to themselves.

"Mr. Takaishi on Mount Fudō—his cow died. It was a good old cow." The priest was unlike the man I had met at the party in Tokyo. With a cup or so of *sake* in him, he was flushed down to his neck as he spoke to Mr. Nakamura. Over the course of the day, he and Jirō had perhaps ceased to regard me as an outsider. Gradually I warmed to this countrified priest, so unlike the swaggering prelates of Tokyo.

"Are there any *kakure* on Mount Fudō?" I asked.

"None. Everyone there belongs to our parish." He thrust out his chest a bit as he spoke, and Jirō and Nakamura nodded solemnly. I had noticed that morning how these people seemed to look down upon the *kakure* and regard them with contempt.

"There's nothing we can do about them. They won't have anything to do with us. Those people behave like some kind of secret society."

The *kakure* of Gotō and Ikitsuki were no longer as withdrawn as those on this island. Here even the Catholics appeared to be wary of the secretiveness of the *kakure.* But Jirō and Mr. Nakamura had *kakure* among their ancestors. It was rather amusing that the two of them now seemed to be oblivious of that fact.

"What exactly do they worship?"

"What do they worship? Well, it's no longer true Christianity." The priest sighed in consternation. "It's a form of superstition."

They gave me another interesting piece of information. The Catholics on the island celebrate Christmas and Easter according to the Western calendar, but the *kakure* secretly continue to observe the same festivals according to the old lunar calendar.

"Once when I went up the mountain, I found them all gathered together on the sly. Later I asked around and discovered they were celebrating their Easter."

After Nakamura and Jirō left, I returned to my room. My head felt feverish, perhaps due to the *sake,* and I opened the window. The ocean was pounding like a drum. Darkness had spread thickly in all directions. It seemed to me that the drumming of the waves deepened the darkness and the silence. I have spent nights in many different places, but I have never known a night as fathomless as this.

I was moved beyond words as I reflected on the many long years that the *kakure* on this island would have listened to the sound of this ocean. They were the offspring of traitors who had abandoned their religious beliefs because of the fear of death and the infirmities of their flesh. Scorned by the officials and by the Buddhist laity, the *kakure* had moved to Gotō, to Ikitsuki, and here to this island. Nevertheless, they had been unable to cast off the teachings of their ancestors, though they did not have the courage to defend their faith boldly like the martyrs of old. They had lived amid their shame ever since.

Over the years, that shame had shaped the unique features of their faces. They were all the same—the four or five men who had ridden with me on the ferry boat, Jirō, and Mr. Nakamura. Occasionally a look of duplicity mingled with cowardice would dart across their faces.

Although there were minor differences between the *kakure* village organizations on this island and those in the settlements on Gotō or Ikitsuki, in each village the role of the priest was filled by either the "Watchman" or the "Village Elder." The latter would teach the people the essential prayers and important festival days. Baptism was administered to newly born infants by the "Waterworks Official." In some villages the positions of "Village Elder" and "Waterworks Official" were assumed by the same individual. In many instances these offices had been passed down through the patriarchal line for many generations. On Ikitsuki I had observed a case where units of organization had been established for every five households.

In front of the officials, the *kakure* had of course pretended to be practicing Buddhists. They belonged to their own parish temples and had their names recorded as Buddhist believers in the religious registry. Like their ancestors, at certain times they were forced to trample on the *fumie* in the presence of the authorities.[1] On the days when they had trodden on the sacred image, they returned to their vil-

1. *Fumie:* A picture of Christ or Mary with the Babe rendered on paper or metal. Japanese authorities used it during the age of Christian persecution from the seventeenth through nineteenth centuries to test whether a person would step on the image to prove they were not Christian.

lages filled with remorse over their own cowardice and filthiness, and there they scourged themselves with ropes woven of fibers, which they called *tempensha.* The word originally meant "whip," and was derived from their misinterpretation of the Portuguese word for "scourge." I have seen one of these *tempensha* at the home of a Tokyo scholar of the Christian era. It was made from forty-six strands of rope, woven together, and did in fact cause a considerable amount of pain when I struck my wrist with it. The *kakure* had flogged their bodies with such whips.

Even this act of penitence did not assuage their guilt. The humiliation and anxiety of a traitor does not simply evaporate. The relentless gaze of their martyred comrades and the missionaries who had guided them continued to torment them from afar. No matter how diligently they tried, they could not be rid of those accusing eyes. Their prayers are therefore unlike the awkwardly translated Catholic invocations of the present day; rather they are filled with faltering expressions of grief and phrases imploring forgiveness. These prayers, uttered from the stammering mouths of illiterate *kakure,* all sprang from the midst of their humiliation. "Santa Maria, Mother of God, be merciful to us sinners in the hour of death." "We beseech thee, as we weep and moan in this vale of tears. Intercede for us, and turn eyes filled with mercy upon us."

As I listened to the thrashing of the sea in the darkness, I thought of the *kakure,* finished with their labors in the fields and their fishing upon the waters, muttering these prayers in their rasping voices. They could only pray that the mediation of the Holy Mother would bring forgiveness of their frailties. For to the *kakure,* God was a stern paternal figure, and as a child asks its mother to intercede with its father, the *kakure* prayed for the Virgin Mary to intervene on their behalf. Faith in Mary was particularly strong among the *kakure,* and I concluded that their weakness had also prompted them to worship a figure that was a composite of the Holy Mother and Kannon, the Buddhist Goddess of Mercy.

I could not sleep even after I crawled into bed. As I lay beneath the thin coverlet, I tried to sing the words of the song that Jirō had performed that evening, but I couldn't remember them.

* * *

I had a dream. It seemed that my operation was over and I had just been wheeled back to my room; I lay back on the bed like a dead man. A rubber tube connected to an oxygen tank was thrust into my nostril, and transfusion needles from the plasma bottles hung over my bed had been inserted into my right arm and leg. My consciousness should have been blurred, but I recognized the grayish shadow that clutched my hand. It was my mother, and she was alone with me in my hospital room. There were no doctors; not even my wife.

I saw my mother in other places, too. As I walked over a bridge at dusk, her face would sometimes appear suddenly in the gathering clouds overhead. Occasionally I would be in a bar, talking with the hostesses; when the conversation broke off and a sense of empty meaninglessness stole across my heart, I would feel my mother's presence beside me. As I bent over my work desk late in the night, I would abruptly sense her standing behind me. She seemed to be peering over my shoulder at the movements of my pen. I had strictly forbidden my children and even my wife to disturb me while I was working, but strangely it did not bother me to have my mother there. I felt no irritation whatsoever.

At such times, the figure of my mother that appeared to me was not the impassioned woman who had played her violin in search of the one perfect note. Nor was it the woman who had groped for her rosary each morning on the first Hankyū-line train, deserted except for the conductor. It was rather a figure of my mother with her hands joined in front of her, watching me from behind with a look of gentle sorrow in her eyes.

I must have built up that image of my mother within myself, the way a translucent pearl is gradually formed inside an oyster shell. For I have no concrete memory of ever seeing my mother look at me with that weary, plaintive expression.

I now know how that image came to be formed. I superimposed on her face that of a statue of "Mater Dolorosa," the Holy Mother of Sorrows, which my mother used to own.

After my mother's death, people came to take away her kimonos and obis and other possessions one after another. They claimed to be sharing out mementoes of my mother, but to my young eyes, my aunts seemed to be going through the drawers of her dresser like shoppers rifling through goods in a department store. Yet they paid no attention to her most valued possessions—the old violin, the well-used prayer book she had kept for so many years, and the rosary with a string that was ready to break. And among the items my aunts had left behind was that cheap statue of the Holy Mother, the sort sold at every church.

Once my mother was dead, I took those few precious things with me in a box every time I moved from one lodging house to another. Eventually the strings on the violin snapped and cracks formed in the wood. The cover was torn off her prayer book. And the statue of Mary was burned in an air raid in the winter of 1945.

The sky was a stunning blue the morning after the air raid. Charred ruins stretched from Yotsuya to Shinjuku, and all around the embers were still smoldering. I crouched down in the remains of my apartment building in Yotsuya and picked through the ashes with a stick, pulling out broken bowls and a dictionary that had only a few unburned pages remaining. Eventually I struck something hard. I reached into the still warm ashes with my hand and pulled out the broken upper half of that statue. The plaster was badly scorched, and the plain face was even uglier than before. Today, with the passage of time the facial features have grown vaguer. After I was married, my wife once dropped the statue. I repaired it with glue, with the result that the expression on the face is all the more indistinct.

When I went into hospital, I placed the statue in my room. After the first operation failed and I began my second year in hospital, I had reached the end of my rope both financially and emotionally. The doctors had all but given up hope for my recovery, and my income had dissolved to nothing.

At night, beneath the dim lights, I would often stare from my bed at the face of the Holy Mother. For some reason her face seemed sad, and she appeared to be returning my gaze. It was unlike any Western painting or sculpture of the Mother of God that I had ever seen. Its face was cracked from age and from the air raid, and it was missing its nose; where the face had once been, only sorrow remained. When I studied in France, I saw scores of statues and portraits of the "Mater Dolorosa," but this memento of my mother had lost all traces of its origins. Only that sorrow lingered.

At some point I must have blended together the look on my mother's face and the expression on that statue. At times the face of the Holy Mother of Sorrows seemed to resemble my mother's face when she died. I still remember clearly how she looked laid out on top of her quilt, with that shadow of pain etched into her brow.

Only once did I ever tell my wife about my mother appearing to me. The one time I did say something, she gave some sort of reply, but a look of evident displeasure flickered on her face.

* * *

There was fog everywhere.

The squawking of crows could be heard in the mist, so we knew that the village was near at hand. With my reduced lung capacity, it was quite a struggle to make it all this way. The mountain path was very steep, but my greatest difficulty was that the boots which Jirō had lent me kept slipping in the sticky clay.

Even so, Mr. Nakamura explained, we were having an easier time of it than in the old days. Back then—and we couldn't see it now because of the fog—there had been just one mountain path to the south, and it had taken half a day to reach the village. The resourceful *kakure* had deliberately chosen such a remote location for their village in order to avoid surveillance by the officials.

There were terraced fields on both sides of the path, and the black silhouettes of trees emerged from the fog. The shrieking of the crows grew louder. I remembered the flock of crows that had circled the summit of the Isle of Rocks on the previous day.

Mr. Nakamura called out to a mother and child working in the fields. The mother removed the towel that covered her face and bowed to him politely.

"Kawahara Kikuichi's house is just down this way, isn't it?" Nakamura asked. "There's a Sensei from Tokyo here who'd like to talk to him."

The woman's child gawked at me curiously until his mother scolded him, at which point he charged off into the field.

It had been Mr. Nakamura's sensible suggestion that we bring along a bottle of *sake* from the village as a gift for Mr. Kawahara. Jirō had carried it for me on our trek, but at this point I took it from him and followed the two men into the village. A radio was playing a popular song. Some of the houses had motorcycles parked in their sheds.

"All the young people want to get out of this place."

"Do they come to town?"

"No, a lot of them go to work in Sasebo or Hirado. I suppose it's hard for them to find work on the island when they're known as children of the *kakure*."

The crows were still following us along the road. They settled on the thatched roof of a house and cawed. It was as if they were warning the villagers of our arrival.

The house of Kawahara Kikuichi was somewhat larger than the others in the village, with a tiled roof and a giant camphor tree growing at the back. A single look at the house and it was obvious Kikuichi was the "Village Elder," the individual who performed the role of priest in this community.

Leaving me outside, Mr. Nakamura went into the house

and negotiated with the family for a few minutes. The child we had seen in the field watched us from a distance, his hands thrust into trousers that had half fallen down. I glanced at him and realized that his bare feet were covered with mud. The crows squawked again.

I turned to Jirō. "It looks as though he doesn't want to meet us."

"Oh, no. With Mr. Nakamura talking to him, everything will be just fine," he reassured me.

Finally an agreement was reached. When I stepped inside the earthen entranceway, a woman was staring at me from the dark interior. I held out the bottle of *sake* and told her it was a small token of my gratitude, but there was no response.

Inside the house it was incredibly dark. The weather was partly to blame, but it was so dark I had the feeling it would be little different on a clear day. And there was a peculiar smell.

Kawahara Kikuichi was a man of about sixty. He never looked directly at me, but always kept his fearful eyes focused on some other spot in the room as he spoke. His replies were truncated, and he gave the impression that he wanted us to leave as soon as possible. Each time the conversation faltered, my eyes shifted to different corners of the room, to the stone mortar in the entranceway, to the straw matting, or to the sheaves of straw. I was searching for the characteristic staff that belonged to the "Village Elder," and for the place where they had concealed their icons.

The Village Elder's staff was something only he was allowed to possess. When he went to perform baptisms, he carried a staff made of oak; to drive evil spirits from a home, he used a silverberry staff. His staff was never made from bamboo. Clearly these staffs were an imitation of the croziers carried by priests in the Christian age.

I searched carefully, but I was unable to locate either a staff or the closet where the icons were hidden away. Eventually I was able to hear the prayers handed down to Kikuichi from his ancestors, but the hesitant expressions of grief and the pleas for forgiveness were like every other *kakure* supplication I had heard.

"We beseech thee, as we weep and moan in this vale of tears." As he intoned the melody, Kikuichi stared into space. "Intercede for us, and turn eyes filled with mercy upon us." Like the song Jirō had crooned the previous evening, this was just a string of clumsy phrases addressed as an appeal to someone.

"As we weep and moan in this vale of tears . . ." I repeated Kikuichi's words, trying to commit the tune to memory.

"We beseech thee . . ."

"We beseech thee."

". . . Turn eyes filled with mercy . . ."

"Turn eyes filled with mercy . . ."

In the back of my mind was an image of the *kakure* returning to their village one night each year after being forced to trample on the *fumie* and pay their respects at the Buddhist altars. Back in their darkened homes, they recited these words of prayer. "Intercede for us, and turn eyes filled with mercy upon us. . . ."

The crows shrieked. For a few moments we were all silent, staring out at the thick mist that drifted past the veranda. A wind must have got up, for the milky fog swirled by more quickly than before.

"Could you perhaps show me your . . . your altar icons?" I stammered through my request, but Kikuichi's eyes remained fixed in another direction, and he gave no answer. The term "altar icons" is not Christian jargon, of course, but refers more generally to the Buddhist deities which are worshipped in an inner room of the house. Among the *kakure,* however, the object to which they prayed was concealed in the most inconspicuous part of the house; to deceive the officials, they referred to these images as their "altar icons." Even today, when they have full freedom of worship, they do not like to show these images to non-believers. Many of them believe that they defile their hidden icons by displaying them to outsiders.

Mr. Nakamura was somewhat firmer in his request. "He's come all the way from Tokyo. Why don't you show them to him?"

Finally Kikuichi stood up.

We followed him through the entranceway. The eyes of the woman in the darkened room were riveted on our movements.

"Watch your head!" Jirō called out from behind as we entered the inner room. The door was so low we had to bend over in order to go in. The tiny room, darker than the entranceway, was filled with the musty smells of straw and potatoes. Straight ahead of us was a small Buddhist altar decorated with a candle. This was certainly a decoy. Kikuichi's eyes shifted to the left. Two pale blue curtains hung there, though I had not noticed them when we came through the door. Rice cakes and a white bottle of offertory wine had been placed on the altar stand. Kikuichi's wrinkled hand slowly drew aside the curtains. Gradually the sections of an ochre-colored hanging scroll were revealed to us.

Behind us, Jirō sighed, "It's just a picture."

A drawing of the Holy Mother cradling the Christ child—no, it was a picture of a farm woman holding a nursing baby. The robes worn by the child were a pale indigo, while the mother's kimono was painted a murky yellow. It was clear from the inept brushwork and composition that the picture had been painted many years before by one of the local *kakure*. The farm woman's kimono was open, exposing her breast. Her obi was knotted at the front, adding to the impression that she was dressed in the rustic apparel of a worker in the fields. The face was like that of every woman on the island. It was the face of a woman who gives suckle to her child even as she ploughs the fields and mends the fishing nets. I was suddenly reminded of the woman earlier who had removed the towel from her face and bowed to Mr. Nakamura.

Jirō had a mocking smile on his face. Mr. Nakamura was pretending to look serious, but I knew that inside he was laughing.

Still, for some time I could not take my eyes off that clumsily drawn face. These people had joined their gnarled hands together and offered up supplications for forgiveness to this portrait of a mother. Within me there welled up the feeling that their intent had been identical to mine. Many long years ago, missionaries had crossed the seas to bring the teachings of God the Father to this land. But when the missionaries had been expelled and the churches demolished, the Japanese *kakure,* over the space of many years, stripped away all those parts of the religion that they could not embrace, and the teachings of God the Father were gradually replaced by a yearning after a Mother—a yearning which lies at the very heart of Japanese religion. I thought of my own mother. She stood again at my side, an ashen-colored shadow. She was not playing the violin or clutching her rosary now. Her hands were joined in front of her, and she stood gazing at me with a touch of sorrow in her eyes.

The fog had started to dissipate when we left the village, and far in the distance we could see the dark ocean. The wind seemed to have stirred up the sea again. I could not see the Isle of Rocks. The mist was even thicker in the valley. From somewhere in the trees that rose up through the mist, crows cried out. "In this vale of tears, intercede for us; and turn eyes filled with mercy upon us." I hummed the melody of the prayer that I had just learned from Kikuichi. I muttered the supplication that the *kakure* continually intoned.

"How ridiculous! Sensei, it must have been a terrible disappointment to have them show you something so stupid." As we left the village, Jirō apologized to me over and over, as though he were personally responsible for the whole thing. Mr. Nakamura, who had picked up a tree branch along the way to use as a walking stick, walked ahead of us in silence. His back was stiff. I couldn't imagine what he was thinking.

A Six-Day Trip

There were a great many koi in the restaurant's miniature pond. While my uncle was discussing something with the hostess, my wife and I stepped out of the tatami dining room and went out into the nighttime gardens. In the pond surrounded by large trees, swarms of koi had formed ranks and were swimming around. Several small koi surrounded a gigantic black koi. They bumped against one another, twisted their bodies, and, from an excess of energy, occasionally some would leap out of the water. They acted like schools of salmon swimming upstream in a river to spawn.

"So you say you're going to write a story about your mother?" My uncle, who taught at a local university, asked as he clumsily tore into the river fish he was eating.

"Not right away. But for some time now I've been thinking that I have to write a story about Mother. But . . ." I smiled in an attempt to gain his approval, "there are many people who would be offended by it who are still living. So I can't write it yet."

"That's true, your mother was an intense woman. We brothers learned a great deal from her, but she also hurt us badly. I can't even count the number of times she severed ties with us."

"But Mom . . . She was a woman who really lived her life. She never lived idly like I do."

A memory of her popped into my head, the way it always did at times like this. A wintry day in Dalian, thirty years ago. Icicles dangled in front of our windows. As I lay back on the sofa, Mother continued playing her violin without a single break. It was already dark in the room. Without turning on the lights, Mother kept repeating a single melody, over and over again. Two hours earlier, I had watched as her chin and neck became engorged with blood, swelling scarlet. And I saw blood dripping from her fingertips. Yet she wouldn't stop. She wouldn't respond even when I called to her. It was enough to frighten me back then.

"I don't have her disposition."

"Neither do I or her other brothers." My uncle forced a smile. "It was just your mother and her younger sister who did."

"I've heard that Aunt Eiko was like that."

I had vague memories of my mother's younger sister, who was a bit older than this uncle.

Maybe it's strange for a nephew to say this, but even as a child I thought that aunt had a strikingly beautiful face. Once, when I was young, she took me to see a festival. I was amazed at how many different kinds of candy she bought me. When we returned home, she got into a fierce argument with my mother because of that. Years later, she was jilted by a man and committed suicide.

"She threw herself off the cliff at Yashima and died, if you can imagine such a thing. The man that such an impassioned woman fell in love with . . . he must have felt a lot like the Priest Anchin from the Dōjōji Temple.[1] No ordinary man could continue to live with her."

I totally agreed with what my uncle said. But it wasn't just my aunt's lover. I'm sure that my father, who was raised in the countryside and went on to study at Tokyo University, was dazzled by the young woman who was studying violin at the Ueno School of Music. I don't yet know what sort of relationship he had with Mother. But I suspect that a man like him, who always wanted to stay on dependable asphalt paths, must not have been able to stand Mother's intensity after they were married. In his later years, my father would often say, "The greatest happiness comes from being ordinary. The greatest happiness comes when nothing at all happens." That was his reaction against the kind of life that Mother lived. After being dragged around by Mother for ten years, all my father wanted after their divorce was to have a secure, simple life that would allow him to forget the past. With nothing at all happening. Just being ordinary. And no doubt the reason he opposed me to the point of intractability when I started to pursue literature was because it distressed him to once again see traces of my mother in his own son. I'm at an age now where I understand why my father abandoned my mother. Even I couldn't imagine living as the husband of such a woman. Yet I hate my father. I shall likely go on hating him for the rest of my life.

1. From the legend of a woman named Kiyohime, which was turned into a famous Noh play in the fifteenth century. Spurned by her lover, Anchin, she pursues him. He conceals himself under the temple bell at Dōjōji Temple, but she turns into a gigantic snake and coils herself around the bell, squeezing until he is consumed by flames.

"Is your father doing well? I haven't seen him for a long time."

"He should be doing fine. But I haven't had any contact with him for years."

"Really?" My uncle set down the cup he had brought to his lips and looked at me in surprise. "Why not?"

With an ambiguous smile, I glanced at my wife, who was sitting next to me. She too was smiling faintly, as though at a loss for words. I suppose she resembled my mother in some ways, and in others was not like her at all. Throughout our trip all she had done was keep phoning our elementary school–aged son we'd left behind in Tokyo. I really don't know why I am so unforgiving of him, even though this was just the sort of woman my father had hoped I would marry. The only thing I'm sure of is the attachment I can't help feeling toward Mother.

"I feel as though I can understand how Dad felt during his college years when he fell in love with Mother, but why would she have loved a man like him?"

"Like him?" My uncle's tone sounded like a rebuke of the heartless judgment I had passed on my own father. "Don't forget that your mother loved a worthless child like you."

"Good point."

I was a bit ashamed. When I step back and put some distance between myself and my father, I can understand him as a man. But when it comes to Mother, I end up idealizing her. That being the case, I hadn't been able to write a story about her no matter how much information about her I could gather.

"How many times did my mother fall in love? At least the cases you know about."

"Three times, maybe? I don't know much about the first one. But I know quite a lot about her relationships with your father and with one other man. It was around the time I was a student at the First Higher School."

"Is it true what I've heard, that because her family wouldn't give her permission to marry Dad, she ran away from home?"

"That wasn't the first time she ran away. She ran off when they wouldn't allow her to attend the music school."

The family in which this uncle and my mother were raised was ruled over by a stern physician living in Kasayama Village, Okayama Prefecture. When Mother graduated from the girls' school in Okayama, she wanted to attend the Ueno School of Music, but neither my grandfather nor my grandmother would give her permission. Six months after graduating from the girls' school, she abruptly disappeared from the family home. I was told that she went into service as a maid in Tokyo in order to get the money for her tuition. I heard this from Mother herself while she was still alive.

"The second time she ran away was while she was living with my older brother. She was living at the time with my brother and his wife. One day she just up and disappeared. Everyone knew where she had gone. When they checked the boarding house where your father was living while he attended the University of Tokyo, she was there with him."

"Impressive!" I glanced with pride toward my wife. "Makes me want to brag about having a mother like that."

"But imagine having someone like that as your mother-in-law . . . It would have been hell."

"What about her third love affair . . . Who was the man?"

I had gotten a little too caught up in the story. My uncle's face clouded over.

"I wonder if I should tell you. It might shock you if I told you."

"Why? Finding out a secret from my mother's past?"

"I just thought it might destroy the image you have of your mother. Oh, I'll just go ahead and tell you. It was your dad's older brother."

"What?"

I swallowed hard. I had never heard any such thing. I'd never met Dad's older brother.

After he graduated from a foreign language school, I understand he traveled to Brazil, and I heard that while he was doing land reclamation deep in the Amazon, he disappeared without a trace.

"Is that my uncle who went to Brazil?"

"It is. Your mother made up her mind to follow him to Brazil. But she gave up the idea. For various reasons."

"Did Dad know about all this?"

"Yes, he did."

"*The greatest happiness comes from being ordinary. The greatest happiness comes when nothing at all happens.*" I could almost see his slender face and his timid little eyes as he repeated those familiar words. Connecting his words with the story I had just heard from my uncle, I felt I was starting to understand.

"Why did Dad's brother go to Brazil in the first place?"

"I think it must have been because he felt guilty toward your dad. No, maybe it was more like the way the Priest Anchin felt when he fled from Kiyohime. All my sisters were like that when they were in love with a man. Your mother had no boundaries. She'd go all out, overcoming every obstacle."

"Okay, but the men they loved couldn't handle it, could they?" I mumbled, thinking of the five years I lived with my mother. For five years after she separated from Dad and we moved to Kobe from Dalian, I lived together with Mother, just the two of us. It was during that five-year period that she began choosing the Catholic faith as her way of life. She even had me get baptized. Afterward, every morning she'd make me go to Mass, no matter what excuses I came up with. Even on mornings in January or February, while all the other children were still burrowed under their warm futon quilts, I was walking in total darkness for over half an hour along a frozen path to accompany my mother to early morning Mass. There was just one French priest performing the Mass in the frigid church, and the only people in attendance besides me and my mother were two old women muttering prayers. It was quite a painful daily ritual for a lazy twelve-year-old, but my mother never let me miss a day.

"You're right. It was too much for the men who lived with them."

"But, Uncle, even you still love my mother, don't you?"

"I do. Looking back now, I do miss her, after all."

That night, my wife and I returned to our lodging, and after crawling into bed, I asked my wife something I had never asked her before.

"How do you . . . how do you feel about my mother?"

My wife never met Mother. She died two years before we were married.

"Well, let's see. I . . . I envy the kind of life your mother led, but I could never live that way."

"Why not?"

"It might make some men happy, but others it would wound just as much. I couldn't stand doing that."

Maybe it was because I'd been drinking, but a bright red flame flickered behind my eyelids. Not unlike the flame that had burned red inside my mother. The lives of every person who encountered that flame were scarred. Some men, like my father, were scorched and reduced to a pitiful pile of ashes, but there were others who burned as bright as she had.

* * *

On the train the next day, I continued to think about what kind of story I could write with my mother as protagonist. But there seemed little likelihood I could write it at the present time. There were several men she had associated with that even my uncle knew nothing about. They were still alive. Furthermore, when I became a novelist, my father gave me strict instructions that I was never to write about him or my family. Having promised him that I wouldn't, there was no way I could write about them even if my father disowned me.

The train raced along the coastline from Fukuoka toward Nagasaki. It was raining, and white waves frothed the sea. I spotted a few summer bungalows and a procession of windbreaks set up with pine groves.

* * *

"The wind seems pretty strong here," my wife said. "Every branch is bent toward us."

Just as she said, the branches of all the short pines in the groves were pointed away from the sea. Their trunks and leaves were all caked white with dust and sand. A truck was parked on the rainswept beach, and two or three men were shoveling gravel.

"These pine trees . . . They're like the men who had to contend with your mother."

It was like what my wife had whispered the night before: my mother either delighted the people around her or wounded them. At the very least, something like a flame inside her left a mark on the lives of those she encountered. If such people had never known her, their lives might have turned out very differently. Just as the winter rain-swept winds changed the direction of those pine trees, Mother changed the direction of the lives of those she met.

"So true, so true," I muttered, and then shook my head. Like my wife, there wasn't any way I could stand such a life. For many years I had felt that the deeds or the sins of one person could decisively change the direction of another person's life, and perhaps that was because I had seen how my mother lived. It was enough for me simply to have my wife and my son. That's probably why I had preferred to live an unexceptional life in spite of my work as a novelist.

After taking care of some business in Nagasaki, we flew to Osaka. We had planned to return directly to Tokyo but decided to stop over in Osaka for two days because I wanted to show my wife the house where I had lived with my mother as a child, along with some other places from my youth. In addition, I wanted to learn a little more about my father's older brother, the one three days earlier my uncle had told me was my mother's third lover. That man's son lived in Osaka. Although he was my cousin, I had scarcely had any contact with him. Especially after I broke off my relationship with my father, he had become like a total stranger to me.

Even to my eyes, the Osaka-Kobe region that I was visiting for the first time in many years had completely changed from when I was a youth. The worst change had come to the

Rokkō mountain range that formed the backdrop of the region: the mountains were beginning to be destroyed, exposing the white skin of the slopes. Just like in Tokyo, everywhere you looked housing developers were slicing off the slopes with bulldozers.

The house where I had lived with my mother was still where it had stood. But it, too, no longer looked the way it had back then. And the surrounding area looked nothing like it had in the past. Rows of identical public housing buildings stood where there had once been vacant land, and the trees in the pine groves that had been there had all been felled, replaced by supermarkets and pachinko parlors and medical clinics. The road itself was the only thing that had not changed.

"Every morning," I explained to my wife, "I traveled this road to the church."

My mother would wake up an hour before I got up, and after getting dressed she would pray her rosary in her room. A faint light shown through the window of Mother's room, which was adjacent to my bedroom, and I could see her shadow as she prayed. I would heave a sigh and slowly change into my clothes and go downstairs. In winter, we'd go outside into what seemed like the dead of night, and the road would be icy from frost. The Catholic church was a thirty-minute walk from our home. Along the way Mother would say hardly a word; she continued to pray. Once we finally reached the church, I would sit motionless, battling drowsiness. If I dozed off, Mother would jab me from time to time with her bony elbow. The shadow of the French priest as he bent over the altar was projected on the wall by candlelight. This chapel was filled with believers on Sundays, but on other days, besides me and Mother only two elderly women who took care of the priest attended Mass.

"That must have been hard for you," my wife smiled. "Having to wake up so early. I can't even imagine it given what you're like now."

"It really took a toll on me."

Oddly enough, back then, unlike now, I had a simple faith, and I even seriously considered becoming a priest myself in the future. That of course was nothing more than the fleeting enthusiasm or sentimentality of my youth, but Mother tried to inculcate in me the understanding that the most exalted realm, superior to all others, was the realm of the sacred. The love that she had never been able to attain from men she now grasped for through her studies of religious music, music that had begun to point her toward God. She managed to make ends meet by teaching music at several Catholic girls' schools, but her energies were dedicated less to those schools than to the study of Gregorian chant. Sometimes she would take me to listen to concerts given in Osaka or Kobe. But on our way home afterward, Mother would always talk disdainfully about the performers. "They're no better than technicians. They don't understand what's most important, those people." The musician she most highly respected was her teacher at music school, Andō Kō, the younger sister of the novelist Kōda Rohan.

"Take a look," I said to my wife, pointing to several dilapidated houses nearby. "You might not believe it, but in that house and in some of those over there—my mother converted their families to Christianity."

When we had lived here, there hadn't been more than perhaps twenty houses in the neighborhood. They all belonged to mid-level office workers who commuted to Kobe or Osaka. Their wives had initially watched with suspicion and curiosity as this mother and her son rose early each morning to attend church. Eventually one of the mothers brought her daughter over and asked Mother to teach her the violin. Over time, similar connections formed with more of the mothers. Finally, they began attending church with Mother, and two or three years later they began to be baptized. After this, some of these women's husbands asked to be introduced to the priest. That of course didn't go so well, so Mother urgently raced around preaching Christianity to them. When she died, some of them came all the way to Tokyo and even joined the family mourners who proceeded to the cemetery after the funeral.

"Three of them have passed away by now."

"Then you ought to pay a visit to their cemeteries," my wife said. "They must have treated you very well when you were a child."

The Catholic cemetery was on the grounds next to the church I had attended as a child. So what my wife said made perfect sense. The road I had traversed thirty years earlier with my mother, the morning star behind us, was now tightly lined with housing on both sides, but the church where the French priest had bent over the altar, casting a solitary shadow as he recited the Mass was still as it had been, along with its adjoining cemetery. Since I'd had Mother buried in a Catholic cemetery in Tokyo, her grave was not here, but the French priest, along with three of the men she had brought to the church, all slept beneath the ground here.

* * *

A rather poor copy of the statue of Our Lady of Lourdes stood in the center of the cemetery, with wood or stone grave markers fanning out from that center point. A small dust devil twisted in a corner of the cemetery, kicking up dancing clouds of dust. I joined my hands together and offered a prayer at the grave of the French priest before standing at the graves of Mr. and Mrs. Uchida and Mrs. Kaneda.

"This woman's husband loved me like a father."

"Did he?"

The baptismal name "Peter" was inscribed on the headstone of Mr. Uchida, who had worked for Yamashita Steamship Lines. At first, he was vehemently opposed to his wife attending church. But over time, after his wife was baptized and attended Sunday Mass with my mother, occasionally Mr. Uchida would accompany them. This man and his wife passed away, one after the other, but when I sent a letter of condolence to Mr. Uchida after his wife died, he wrote back, "I'm sure that if your mother hadn't lived in our neighborhood, my life and that of my wife would have taken a very different path."

Looking at his blackened granite headstone I suddenly recalled those words from his letter. The windbreak of trees that we had seen along the coastline two days ago. The pine grove where the branches of the trees had been bent in our direction by the wind. Mother changed the direction of the lives of the Uchidas, Mr. Kaneda, and many others who lived here. She also turned my face toward the Christ in whom I believe. Among their children, one became a seminarian and traveled to Europe to study, while another became a nun in a Trappist convent. (I couldn't imagine anyone except my wife doing something so extreme.)

That afternoon, I decided to visit the family of my father's late brother. "Don't you think they might not like it if we just showed up at their place unannounced?" my wife worried, but I shook my head and said, "Can't help that. I really want to see the traces my mother left in the lives of other people."

From our hotel I phoned my uncle's son, Kōichi. I informally call him "Kōichi," but by rights I should call him "Kōichi-san." But I feel toward this cousin of mine none of the closeness or nostalgia one usually feels toward cousins. I'd hardly ever seen him before.

"Why did it turn out that way?"

"Why? Well, for some reason my father was estranged from his brother's family for years. No, it wasn't just 'some reason.' I finally understand now the reason for the estrangement . . ."

* * *

It wasn't Kōichi-san but his wife who answered the phone. From her raspy voice I envisioned a woman with a dark complexion, perhaps with a soiled bandage wrapped around her neck.

"Actually, he's in the hospital."

"In the hospital?"

"He has heart problems, okay?"

We got the address of the hospital from her, and after I had my wife buy a fruit basket, we set out for the southern edge of Osaka. It was near evening, and the western sun shone on the Nara Highway, where the traffic inched along thanks to all the trucks and cars, which irritated me. The taxi driver kept apologizing, saying this was very unusual.

Kōichi-san's room was on the second floor of a private hospital. The walls along the corridor were stained. We could hear children singing on the road outside. Surprised at this unexpected visit, my cousin lifted his swollen brown face to look up at us, and no matter how many times we asked him to lay back, he sat up on his bed looking embarrassed.

"So, do you come to Osaka occasionally?" he asked in a soft voice. I thought of his wife's harsh, raspy voice on the phone and answered, "No, not very often." Kōichi-san did not respond, merely stared at the fruit basket we had brought.

"How many years has it been since your father died?"

"It's been thirty years."

"So you were still young. And they never found his body?"

"Never did. He got drunk and disappeared into the forest."

This uncle of mine had kept on drinking in spite of all the people around him that tried to get him to stop. According to Kōichi-san, the liquor was of inferior quality, and in his final years he chugged down the strong local alcohol that the natives drank, ruining his stomach. On that fateful day, he got drunk and staggered into the woods. I suppose that's why he lost his way. He had never once returned to Japan, and kept saying he didn't ever want to go back.

"It didn't matter how many times my mother asked him to come back to Japan, he went on insisting he didn't want to."

I looked at Kōichi-san's sallow face. But there was no particular change in his expression.

It didn't appear that he knew anything about the relationship between his father and my mother. After my uncle went to Brazil, he married a waitress who worked at a Japanese restaurant in São Paulo.

"Please take care of yourself," I said, and left his darkened room. Sitting upright on his bed with both hands resting on his lap, Kōichi-san bent his slender neck in a bow, as though relieved that we were leaving. On our way out, we nearly bumped into a nurse who was bringing him his dinner.

* * *

Although there was no proof that they had had an affair, as I walked down the darkened stairs that reeked of cresol, I conjured up the face of a man that my mother had made miserable. In Brazil he had kept drinking, insisting that he would never return to Japan, where his brother and sister-in-law were living. He disappeared into the forest and was never seen again. Maybe that wasn't my mother's fault. But just as there was no proof of that, neither was there any evidence to the contrary. Still, if Mother hadn't been part of his life, he would probably never have gone to Brazil. Perhaps he would have had a happy marriage and lived a peaceful life in his waning years. And unlike how Kōichi-san had wound up, his son wouldn't have tried like his father had to run a restaurant that teetered on the verge of bankruptcy, but would have graduated from a university and become a businessman. The wind had twisted one tree, shifting the direction of its branches. That man who had been involved with Aunt Eiko, who threw herself off a cliff at Yashima—what sort of life was he living now? Mother was the younger sister of such a woman. I can't begin to imagine that my uncle, who had been loved by a woman like Mother who threw herself at him, had been spared any wounds to his heart.

The following day was Sunday. My wife and I went to that church for Mass. The church with a steeple and cross imitating the Gothic style didn't seem that impressive to my wife, but memories from my youth permeated its walls and even the oleanders in the garden. The door to the sanctuary was the same door I had pushed open on wintry mornings when I had to blow on my hands, numb from the cold, and the kneelers were just as they had been when I tried not to let Mother catch me dozing off. One difference now was that a young Japanese priest was saying the Mass in place of the French priest, who when he bent over the altar cast a shadow on the walls that resembled a skinny bird. And the seats now were filled with believers. Faces unfamiliar to me, faces who did not recognize me, the faces of students and young women singing the Gregorian chants my mother had so loved. Businessmen with their wives and children. Among the worshipers there was even a young man dressed in the uniform of the Self-Defense Forces. I stared at the backs of these people, searching for anyone I knew.

There were in fact people there who I knew, but evidently I had forgotten that, just as I had gotten older, they were now old men and women. When they received the host and returned to their seats with their eyes lowered, I finally recognized that it was Mr. Tanaka, and Mr. and Mrs. Nakagami. Each of them had been younger then than I was now. And it was none other than my mother who had initially brought them to this church.

"Oh!!"

After Mass, when Mrs. Nakagami looked up at me after she noticed me in front of her, her deeply wrinkled face twisted into a smile. I was quickly surrounded by Mr. Tanaka, Mr. Nakagami, and Mr. Kagawa, who patted my shoulders or shook my hand.

"We've all seen you on TV. We always watch when you're on TV," Mrs. Nakagami clutched my hand and said in a loud voice that made me blush. "If your mother had still been alive when you started appearing on television, she really might have ended up on those shows herself."

The students and young women who had been singing in the choir grinned as they watched me from a distance. I searched the puffy eyelids and wrinkled cheeks in the aged faces of Mr. Tanaka and Mr. Nakagami for the traces my mother had left there. It had been Mother who had introduced the light of Christ into the hearts of these people. But I wondered how she had felt about those other men who would not have been so miserable had she not been a part of their lives.

* * *

About a month after we returned to Tokyo, I was passing through Shibuya in a car. When I reached Kamitōri, a misty rain began to dampen my windshield, and fearing that my tires might slip, I slowed down and began a slow descent down the slope at Dōgenzaka. An elderly man wearing a fedora stood in the drizzling rain, searching in vain for a taxi. It was my father.

Not once since I had broken off with him had I wanted to talk with him or even see his face, but during these five years he had lost a great deal of weight, and it looked as though his shoulders had stooped. For a brief moment, I felt nothing for him but pity. But I jammed my foot down on the accelerator to crush that feeling out of existence. My car glided past my father as he stood at the edge of the sidewalk, and for just an instant I had a close look at him in his fedora, but the image quickly vanished.

Spring in Galilee

We were told that Jerusalem in March was balmy, like the climate at a summer retreat. But after the taxi we were finally able to hire at the Tel Aviv airport drove through a village lined with barracks and came to a field where giant clouds cast their shadows, we began to see craggy mountains still blotched with snow. It quickly turned chilly inside the taxi, and my legs and those of my wife began shaking. I had caught a cold in Rome, so I pulled a muffler from the bag at my feet and wound it around my neck, staring at what looked like rusted scrap metal scattered across the mountainsides. The driver, who until then had remained silent, suddenly began talking in French.

"During the war, a suicide corps delivered food to the Israeli troops who were left to die in Jerusalem, and what you see over there is the wreckage of their trucks. They were attacked here by Arab forces, and they say that over half the convoy was destroyed."

When I told my wife what he had said, she continued to shake as she asked, "Really? How frightening! Was that recently?" I translated her question for the driver, but he embarrassed us when he shook his head indignantly and replied that this heroic incident happened many years ago, during the first Palestinian War.

As we neared Jerusalem, we came to two checkpoints. At each, a helmeted soldier raised his hand to stop the taxi. Both soldiers had the pleasant faces of young men, and when they learned we were Japanese, they apologized politely, "Excuse me."

As we crossed over a mountain, Jerusalem suddenly appeared on a high plateau in the distance. It was still a new city, with white, modern-looking structures and row upon row of apartment buildings. It was a city built by Israel, and ancient Jerusalem, buried deep inside, was nowhere to be seen from our vantage point. Strips of evening light streamed down on the city from breaks in the clouds.

It had been a lifelong dream of mine to visit this Holy City. I was deeply moved and became quite emotional.

"We're . . . we're finally here, aren't we?" I muttered, not so much to my wife, who was still shivering from the cold, as to myself. But when I say I muttered to myself—and this is connected to my own faith—for all intents and purposes I was speaking to my late mother. My faith, if indeed it can be called faith, is linked to my attachment to my mother. I am no longer able to think of the faith she turned to after her divorce from my father, and which she tried to encourage in me, without associating it with my memories of and love for her.

"We're . . . we're finally here, aren't we?" I was saying it to my mother. How fervently she had longed to visit this Holy City during her lifetime! Of course, that grand dream had been impossible for her to realize, since she died all alone shortly after the war. Accordingly, we had come here carrying in the luggage at our feet not just notepads and books, but also a weathered photograph of her.

* * *

Our hotel was in the heart of a sector in Israel known as the New City. Since we arrived on the Sabbath, a holy day strictly observed in Judaism, my wife and I returned to our hotel after only a short walk. Every single shop along the main shopping street had closed its shutter doors, and the street itself was as empty as a desert; the only sign of life was a procession of guards dressed in green military uniforms bearing rifles on their shoulders. Following an insipid dinner that reeked of olive oil, we decided to defer serious sightseeing to the next day, and my wife wrote some postcards while I began searching a map of Israel, repeatedly referring back to books and the Bible to determine places we would visit tomorrow.

Even with the land area that Israel had seized from the Arabs in the most recent war, Israel was at best only the size of the island of Kyushu, and I had really no interest in seeing kibbutzim or desert agricultural production. All that I wanted to visit were the villages and hillsides and seas that my mother and I had read about time after time in the New Testament when I was a boy. I decided that on the first and second days, we would see Jerusalem and Bethlehem and Bethany. On days three and four, we would rent a car and, after crossing over the plains of Judea, we would visit Jericho, the River Jordan, and the remains of a monastery at Qumran famed for the discovery of the Dead Sea Scrolls; day five we would head north toward Nazareth and the Sea of Galilee. That was pretty much the itinerary I devised.

It was so quiet at night in Jerusalem that it was almost hard to believe it was a major city. A dim electric light illuminated the worn copy of the Bible that rested on the bed table tray that I used as a desk. It was the Bible that my mother kept at her bedside until she passed away; I had used it after her, so both the front and back covers were torn and my wife had had to repair them with cellophane tape and cardboard. The passages that my mother had underlined while she was alive leapt out at me as I flipped through the pages, between which she had inserted several sacred pictures. These were depictions of Christ or the Blessed Mother that believers gifted to one another on such holy days as Christmas or Easter.

I examined those sacred images one by one while my wife took a bath. One was a painting of the stable where Jesus was born; another was of Jesus partaking of the Last Supper with His disciples. The composition and execution in both were poorly done, so I assumed they must have been drawn by third-rate artists. On the backside of the pictures was the signature of Father Murant. He was the parish priest of the Shukugawa church who baptized both my mother and me. During the war, he had been placed in an Internment camp as a foreigner from an enemy nation.

My mother had often underlined the sayings that Jesus spoke in Galilee as recorded in the Gospels of Mark and Luke. In addition to her underlining, she had gone so far as to circle in red pencil some of the words He had spoken to the woman with a twelve-year issue of blood or in His well-known Sermon on the Mount.

I could hear the sound of hot water flowing in the bathroom as I stretched out on the bed and, in honor of our visit to the Holy City that my mother had yearned to see, I once again read verses that I had pretty much memorized:

> Blessed are the poor in spirit: for theirs is the kingdom of heaven.
> Blessed are the meek: for they shall possess the land.
> Blessed are they that mourn: for they shall be comforted.
> Blessed are the clean of heart: for they shall see God.

Mother had circled that last verse, "Blessed are the clean of heart," in red. I opened the window and looked outside. Faint lights shone from the building opposite our hotel and the houses on either side of it. On the street below, a lone man was walking, his feet clacking so loudly he might have been wearing wooden shoes.

* * *

I couldn't understand the climate in Israel. When I awoke the next morning, light from a dazzling sun that seemed to have forgotten how cold it had been the previous day flowed into every corner of the street, which was packed with people and automobiles, probably because the Sabbath had ended. Even though it was wartime, a wide range of goods was on display in every store's show window.

I decided we would visit Bethany before seeing Jerusalem. I wanted to follow along every pathway where Jesus had walked on the day prior to and on the day of His execution.

The bus was filled with Arabs, and scarcely had it left the city and traveled a short distance through a wilderness area blanketed with olive trees than we arrived at the village of Bethany. As we wandered aimlessly around the streets with ultraviolet rays stinging our eyes, we were approached by an Arab man, his head wrapped in a dirty cloth, who begged for money.

In this town as silent as death, dark shadows cast by the white houses fell onto the ground, and the pitch black window openings cut into their walls looked like the eyes of a blind man. The house of Mary and Martha that Jesus was fond of visiting had been in this village, but of course there was no chance it could still be seen today. The beggar offered to show us the grave of Lazarus. As my wife crouched down and disappeared into the sham cave, ignoring my grumbling that we were wasting our time, I stared at the stony road that descended into Jerusalem. The road made its way past an Arab graveyard and sloped down through dusty olive fields. A woman was walking along the road, barefoot with a basket balanced on her head. If this road had actually been here since ancient times, Jesus would have taken it on His way to Jerusalem on the day before His death.

When my wife emerged from the cave, her hair was matted with spiderwebs. Holding her nose, she muttered, "It smelled so awful . . . I wish I hadn't gone in."

* * *

We left Bethany and headed to see the house where Jesus partook of the Last Supper with His disciples, when all of a sudden I remembered the holy images I had viewed in our hotel the previous night, and I thought about Father Murant, who had sent them to my mother. Perhaps I thought of him because as I walked along, I had been pondering Judas's state of mind during the Last Supper. Sometime during their lifetime, depending on their age, every Christian feels the way Judas felt. A young person feels as a young Judas might feel; an adolescent experiences what an adolescent Judas did; and now for me, a man past the age of forty, Judas's feelings as he approached old age lurk in the hidden depths of my consciousness.

The Father Murant I knew when I was in middle school must have been thirty-five or -six years old, but he looked older because of his chestnut-colored beard that resembled the one Jesus wore. But his most striking feature was his slightly sunken eyes, like those of Jesus in religious iconography; my mother claimed, "His eyes are clear because his heart is clear," but in reality, I knew that I was constantly being watched by those wine-colored eyes. I felt they saw into the deepest chambers of my own heart.

Father Murant was assigned to our church when I was in my third year at middle school. After the elderly Japanese priest who had been at our church fell ill and was no longer able to work, Father Murant came to us from the leprosy hospital at Gotemba, but no sooner had his transfer been announced than my mother and some of her friends somehow picked up on information about him.

"In any case, he lived alongside the lepers and gave his all to them," my mother informed me. "That's not something an ordinary priest could do."

I learned nearly everything about his career before he even arrived. Immediately upon arriving in Japan he requested the opportunity to work at the leper hospital; just seeing his face, even the most seriously ill patients ceased their groaning; thanks to his influence, the number of patients who were baptized increased sharply—I heard these things from my mother and her friends, feeling mildly uneasy as I listened.

It was more than a little troubling for me to have this

priest assigned to our church. It was around that time that I began losing the faith that I had so innocently possessed in my childhood. In my mother's presence I of course continued to attend Mass and confession as I had before, and even pretended to continue with my morning and evening prayers, but I was a different young man at school. There I hid the fact that I was a Christian, shared vulgar stories with my classmates, and thought nothing of stopping by a café on my way home from school to have a cigarette.

Because the previous Japanese priest was a lot like an aging donkey, good-natured and the very picture of virtue, there was no way he could have been aware of what was happening inside me, and he wholly believed that I was a fine young man merely because I pretended to pray at Mass and helped out at church bazaars.

"Do you . . . do you think you might like to go to a seminary and become a priest?" One day my mother, beaming with happiness, relayed to me the old priest's question. "Although he said he wanted to respect your feelings about it."

I was elated when I heard that. Up until then it had been burdensome for me to be so completely trusted by him, but still there was no reason to feel disturbed by it. At the same time I felt an inward urge to smile at the absurdity of the whole situation.

But with Father Murant's arrival, there was a possibility that he might see right through me. That began to unnerve me. My mother said that those with clean hearts can see into the minds of others, and I was inclined to believe her.

* * *

"This is amazing! So the house where the Last Supper took place is still standing. This will make it worth coming to

Jerusalem." My wife completely swallowed what the guidebooks said about historical remains. She was convinced that the sites we were planning to visit, like the house of the Last Supper, were just as they had been described in the Bible. I was about to say it was no different from the legend of Yoshitsune's pine tree chair, but I kept my mouth shut.[1] Having paid the exorbitant costs to bring her here, there was no need to go out of my way to disillusion her.

The house was not far from Mount Zion, where a United Nations lookout post was located. The walls of the lookout were pockmarked from bullets fired in the recent war. This is the area originally occupied by Jordanian troops that came under fierce attack from the Israeli army.

I clearly remember the first time I met Father Murant. It was Easter Sunday, and the cherry trees at the rear of the church were in full bloom. The members, packed so tightly next to each other in the church that we were bathed in sweat, were more on edge than usual while we knelt as he conducted the Mass.

After the Mass everyone gathered in the garden to welcome the new priest; my mother and her friends were busily serving tea.

The priest was surrounded by the church's board members as people came to greet him. My mother marched me up to him and introduced me as her son.

He peered at me with those slightly sunken, wine-colored eyes but made no attempt to speak to me.

1. The fabled warrior Minamoto no Yoshitsune (circa 1159–1189) won many victories in his clan's battle against the Taira clan, but even so, he incurred the wrath of his older brother, Yoritomo. Tradition has it that, fleeing from Yoritomo, he rested on a pine tree chair en route to Hiraizumi in northern Japan.

Thinking back on it now, I don't suppose he bore me any ill will at the time. But I felt as though I had been snubbed, and my pride was wounded. After all, when the next woman in line brought her little boy to meet him, the priest patted him on the head and picked him up, announcing to everyone that he had a nephew just like him. The child appeared to have taken quite a dislike to the priest's beard and flailed his arms and legs, which caused everyone to give a fawning laugh. Their laughter greatly displeased me.

"It's because you didn't give him a proper greeting." My mother also seemed displeased with what had just happened and scolded me in a low voice as I stood there in misery.

Beginning the next day, she forced me to wake up early every day and took me to morning Mass. She wanted to prove that her son was such a good young man that the previous aged priest had encouraged him to attend a seminary. Seeking to prove myself, I wanted to display my counterfeit prayers even more fervently. Yet, when my mother and I left the church after Mass, the priest never said anything beyond "Good morning" as he walked through the garden.

The house of the Last Supper was a tiny building in the style of a Jewish synagogue. In front of the iron gate five or six French and Italian tourists had assembled, eagerly pressing the record buttons of their 8-millimeter cameras. A guide came out, with a three-corner cap on his head like those worn by Waseda University students, and led us into the building.

"In this room, Jesus partook of the Last Supper along with his twelve disciples, including Judas." He leaned forward with conviction as he surveyed the group. "This was just before the Passover, and here He took a towel and girded

Himself with it, then poured water into a basin and washed the feet of His disciples."

"Liar," I whispered to my wife as we stood at the rear of the other tourists, making sure they didn't hear me. She widened her eyes and studied the walls littered with graffiti and the pillars resembling those in a church, then hesitantly ran her fingers along them. She was truly moved, confident that Jesus had once walked across this floor and knelt here. Her posture reminded me of a chicken pecking at feed, and I had to restrain myself from bursting out laughing. I had never read any book proving that this was the house where the Last Supper took place.

The first time I went to confession with Father Murant was the most anxious time for me. Confession, after all, was a duty required of all Catholics, and we were supposed to confess to the priest every one of the sins we had committed.

Confessions were made in a tiny corner of the church sectioned off with a curtain; in the middle of the space was a stand with a metal lattice, on either side of which the priest and the believer faced one another.

I had concealed my true self from the previous old Japanese priest. Not once had I told him, even in confession, that I smoked cigarettes and looked at lewd photographs. I never revealed anything that my mother might find out about, and the old priest never questioned me any further about my confessions.

The first time I was left alone with Father Murant in that tiny confessional, I felt as though I was shrinking in fear as those hollow, wine-colored eyes stared at me while he intoned a Latin prayer.

I sat in silence until he said, "Well then?" encouraging

me to hurry and start my confession. Just then, I realized that his ears were far too big for his face. That made me feel those ears would not miss a single word I uttered.

"Well then, begin."

I laid out innocuous sins—I hadn't done my homework; I had been lazy at saying my prayers. A single photograph that I had hidden in my desk drawer flashed somewhere in the depths of my brain. In the photograph, dark shadows enfolded the body of a man and the pale body of a woman intertwined like the roots of a tree. I could not mention that photograph to him.

When I said nothing further, he asked, "Is that everything?"

"Yes." Once again he gazed at me with his wine-colored eyes and in a soft voice began to recite the Latin prayer of absolution.

When I finally stepped outside after my confession, the light from the sun seemed to sting my eyes. I felt tremendous self-loathing, and I felt as though I could not endure the presence of Father Murant.

"Then Jesus looked at His disciples and this is what He said." The guide pointed at the door to his right. "'One of you shall betray me . . .' After He had spoken those words you are all familiar with, that is the door through which Judas departed."

At that, the eyes of my wife and of all the other tourists turned as one, like mechanical dolls, toward that doorway.

* * *

The war expanded in China. A new commissioned officer was assigned to our school, and military training for those in their third year or higher became even more rigorous. A growing number of students in my class planned to take exams for the Army or Navy.

One day an unannounced uniform inspection was conducted. All the students were assembled in the schoolyard, and the teachers examined our possessions. Those discovered with cigarettes in their pockets, or those who had photographs of actresses, were forced to stand in a separate line.

From the pile of items at my feet that included my train pass and a handkerchief blackened by my sweat, one of my teachers plucked out a rosary with a crucifix attached to it.

"What the hell is this?" Evidently this physical education teacher had never seen a rosary before.

"You're one of that *Amen* crowd, are you?" For a long while he stared at me suspiciously, then ordered me to stand in the separate line. I ended up standing with those who had been discovered with cigarettes and actress photos, and we were all taken to the teachers' room.

"In your case," the language teacher said, returning my rosary to me, "you don't have anything especially prohibited. But I have to wonder about a family living in this land blessed with an emperor that worships a god of the foreigners."

I felt it was my mother more than myself who was being insulted. Seated across the room, the newly commissioned officer fixed his eyes on me. I bowed to him and left the room.

I hadn't wanted anyone at the school to know I was a Christian. I even felt it would be better to die than to have someone in my school class see me kneeling with my hands joined together in prayer.

Determined not to be mocked as one of the "*Amen* crowd," at school I joined up with the students who went out of their way to avoid any who were the children of believers. There was a group who waved bicycle chains around and picked fights with students at other schools, but I hung out with the clever, sensible crowd.

Since this was the time in our lives when our bodies were changing into those of adults, that was all anyone in our group ever talked about. I began to suffer from the dark, melancholy urges welling up in my body, desires that I could never mention to my mother. But it seemed odd and even painful to me that Father Murant and the people at church continued to wear serene faces, as though they felt none of those desires themselves. To avoid being ridiculed by the others in my group, I went with some of them on my first visit to the red-light district in Nishinomiya, but it made me sick to my stomach when a woman wearing thick white makeup called out to me, and I fled back home. Still, the tiny white face of that woman appeared in my dreams, tormenting me. Each time I peered into the mirror, I felt like I was a truly ugly young man.

In my history class, we had just come to the point where we were studying the closing of the country in the early seventeenth century. The teacher explained that the Christian missionaries came to turn the nations of Asia into colonies of their own countries, that Christianity was a religion created by the white people as a tool to subjugate Asians and Black people, and that it was a good thing that the military government in Japan saw through their plot. The teacher of course had no idea that I was a Christian, but during class I stared at the floor and sank down into my seat so that he wouldn't notice me even for a second.

It was in this manner that I became two different young

men—one while I was at school and the other when I returned home. Neither my mother nor any of her female friends had any clue what was really in my heart. Initially I was very proud of my deceit, but gradually I came to hate myself for what I was doing. Each time I saw my mother's face, my mother who believed in me in every possible way, I was suddenly gripped by the urge to shout to her that I hated going to church.

The reason I was able to stifle that urge was because it pained me to think of wounding my mother.

Father Murant as always ignored me. Thinking about it now, maybe he was instinctively incapable of taking a liking to me. There was no reason for him to love an ugly, dark-skinned, pimple-faced Japanese boy like me.

People without any reason know others that they can't bring themselves to like. Sometimes when I think about Judas, I even wonder if perhaps he had a face that no one instinctively could like. After all, no matter what page you turn to in the Bible, it's clear that Judas was disliked by everyone from the very beginning.

When it became clear to me that Father Murant would never approve of me, a hatred for him began to arise inside me. I started to hope that this man who stared at me with sunken eyes would disclose a weakness like my own, and that if he did, it would allow me to despise him with every fiber of my being.

One day, separated from him in the confessional as always by a metal lattice, after I had with lowered eyes related to him all of my benign sins, he remained silent for a very long time instead of immediately intoning the prayer of absolution. Since no one else was in the church, his silence continued for what seemed like an eternity. Unable to stand it any longer, I said, "That . . . that's everything." I didn't raise my head, but I was painfully aware that those sunken, wine-colored eyes were staring at me. Suddenly, in a soft voice he said, "Are you . . . are you not doing anything to defile yourself?"

Despite the strangeness of his Japanese, I knew immediately what he was asking. Sensing my body shaking, I weakly shook my head.

"Are you sure? Are you not . . . are you not lying to God?"

"I'm not."

At that, in a weary voice he began to mutter the Latin prayer. But I felt as though he had discovered the real me. As I was leaving the church, I felt my forehead bathed in sweat. I loathed the very existence of Father Murant.

* * *

After the Last Supper, Jesus and His eleven disciples left the house. The gates to the city were already closed, and the night had deepened. The group left the city and descended into the Kidron Valley. There were many groves of trees in the valley, so anyone could spend an entire night there without being reprimanded.

In excavations about twenty years ago, a portion of a road that had connected this valley with the city was discovered, and according to several books I had read, this was unquestionably the road that Jesus took on His way to the Garden of Gethsemane.

After lunch, map in hand, my wife and I searched for the road. A short distance to one side we came to the remains of the palace of the High Priest Caiaphas where Jesus was interrogated. Perhaps because it had been buried for so many years, the stone staircase that was unearthed about fifty meters away was broken and cracked here and there.

A profusion of flowers that resembled peaches bloomed beside the staircase. They were covered with clusters of tiny bees. My wife said they were almond blossoms, but her knowledge of flowers cannot be trusted. I sat on the staircase and took photographs of the ruins of Caiaphas's palace off to the right. All that remained there was an ancient church and an old well.

If this really was where Caiaphas's palace had stood, it is the spot where, on that night, Peter had followed after his master and waited until dawn, when the cock crowed three times. Unable to bear the morning chill, he had warmed himself by a fire, and he had stubbornly shaken his head and declared he did not know Jesus.

From the time I passed the age of forty, I was increasingly drawn to this scene in the Bible. I particularly came to like the single line that neither Mark nor John had recorded, but which appeared in the Gospel of Luke. It is a short sentence that comes just as Peter has betrayed Jesus: "And the Lord turning looked on Peter." For some reason, whenever I read this I recall the face of my mother. In my mid-teens, when I announced that I could no longer believe in Christianity, instead of bursting into an angry rage, she stared at me with eyes overflowing with tears, tears that seemed to have emerged from her very depths. To me . . . I feel as though Jesus's eyes when He looked on Peter were just like those eyes of hers.

After that confession day, I could no longer stand Father Murant. He alone had seen through to my true self, and even though it was the duty of a priest to tell no one what he had heard in confession, I felt as though his eyes were always watching me, and it was so abhorrent that I could not bear meeting with him. Even when I pretended to pray in church with my mother, there was no doubt that Father Murant knew that this was only a superficial display.

And then a trivial event occurred in the winter just before I became a fourth-year student in middle school. I was listening along with my mother as Father Murant recited the Mass. Because it was not Sunday, there were only five or six women and an old man who kneeled around us. It was cold and dark inside the church.

The priest was nearly finished with the Mass, and when he bent over the altar and started chanting the final Latin prayer, there was suddenly a loud clatter behind us. When I turned in surprise to see what had happened, a man with piercing eyes and a shaved head, dressed in a national uniform, stood at the doorway while an elderly missionary stopped him from entering.

"Please, just wait a little," the missionary pleaded, on the verge of tears. "The Mass will be over very soon, and we can talk then."

With all our eyes on him, the man squared his shoulders in anger. "Those of you who have come to this church of the foreigners during this time of national emergency—are you really Japanese?!" he shouted.

Father Murant was standing stock still in front of the altar. I looked at him half afraid but even more intensely with a mixture of enjoyment and curiosity. I wanted to see whether he would rebuke the man and throw him out of the church. There was no possibility that the priest did not understand the meaning of the Japanese words that the man had screamed.

But the priest remained motionless, staring toward us with a face contorted in astonishment and fear. I can still clearly remember that face. Even after the man was escorted outside, Father Murant remained frozen before the altar.

I went outside with my mother. The man was nowhere to be seen.

"Let's hurry home," my mother urged me, and we scurried out the church gate as though we were fleeing something.

The next Sunday, a Rising Sun flag stood beside the altar. It had never been there before. In his homily, Father Murant said to us, "We have decided that, starting today, we Christians will join in daily prayer for the soldiers who have gone to war."

* * *

As my wife and I slowly made our way out of the Kidron Valley, an area shaped like a stoneware mortar, a cluster of Arab children begging for money followed doggedly behind us. Each was naked, and one of the girls had a pustule on her lip. Flies swarmed around my sweaty face.

The brown walls surrounding Jerusalem are tall and daunting. I read in some book that these walls in Jesus's day were twice their current size.

I suppose that the soft white hills that lay beyond the valley and the groves of olive trees that dot those hills were the same back in those days. Two pillars resembling anthills that rose up in the direction we were walking marked the tomb of Absalom, who is mentioned in the Old Testament. The Garden of Gethsemane was about a hundred-meter walk beyond Absalom's tomb.

Of course, we can't be certain that even that garden was the spot where Jesus passed the night with His disciples before He was arrested. The speculation that this place was Gethsemane was made in later years, based solely on the coincidental fact that many old olive trees grew there. I said nothing about this to my wife, since there was no need to disillusion her after bringing her all this way to see the Holy Land.

But no matter the exact spot where Jesus awaited His fate that night, it had to have been somewhere in this valley. One scholar has surmised that Judas was well acquainted with the location, it being the place selected for Jesus and His disciples to spend their nights. I could almost envision Jesus staring through the darkness as the light from the torches of the men, led by Judas, approached from the far end of the valley.

In January following the outbreak of war with the United States, Father Murant was unexpectedly apprehended and taken away by Special Police detectives. It was because he was a foreigner from an enemy country.

When I got home from school that day, there was something unusual in the atmosphere of my home. Two or three women were there, telling my mother the circumstances of the priest's arrest as though they had witnessed it themselves.

"You see, he only took one suitcase. The detectives told him that was all he could take, and they quickly put him in their car. Father seems to have been resigned to it all. He just nodded to the missionaries without a word, and off he went."

I raced to the church. The sun was shining as it always did on the church building, and children from the neighborhood were playing outside the gate. The door to the chapel was unlocked, and when I went inside, not a single person was there in the rows of pews. The evening sun shone through the windows to my left, and the whole chamber was vacant and silent.

As I stood there, what I felt, more than surprise that the priest had been arrested by the police, was a kind of liberation—a profound sense of relief that the one person who knew the real me was now gone. My heart swelled with relief that there was no longer a single soul at this church who knew my other self. In an effort to savor this feeling of something like freedom, I sat down in one of the pews and remained there without moving for some time. I could hear nothing other than the sounds of the children playing outside. No flowers decorated the altar at which Father Murant had pronounced the Mass every morning; six candles stood there, seemingly devoid of purpose. It seemed as though I could see infinite specks of dust in the light flowing through the window.

On the fifth day after our arrival in Jerusalem, my wife and I proceeded north. Our goal was to see Jesus's homeland of Nazareth and then walk along the shores of the Sea of Galilee that He had so loved.

Clear days continued one after another, and the calm sea stretched out in front of the kibbutz-managed motel where we stayed. In the morning, we watched as fishermen cast their nets from boats floating in the middle of the sea, just as Peter and his brethren had done. In the evening, the Syrian mountain range that lay beyond the sea was bathed a rosy color in the strong setting sun. We walked around places like Capernaum and Magdala, names familiar to us over many years of reading the Bible.

Near Capernaum was a gently sloping hill. When we approached the hill, we could see a flock of grazing sheep, spread out like spilled milk. A monastery stood at the top of the hill, where we met several nuns who could speak French. According to their explanation, this hill is where Jesus delivered the Sermon on the Mount. "We're here at last," I mumbled to my mother. This was the place mentioned in the Bible that she had most wanted to visit. We sat down on a slope where clover and red flowers bloomed, and I recited to my wife each of the verses in the Sermon on the Mount that my mother had underlined and then circled with a red pencil. "Blessed are the meek," I read, which she followed with "Blessed are the clean of heart."

A Fairy Tale

Once upon a time, many Japanese people lived in a town called Dalian in Manchuria. There were hospitals and government offices and elementary schools that had been built by the Japanese.

In the third-grade class at the elementary school, there was a young boy who was nicknamed Crow. His friends called him Crow because his skin was as dark as that of a great burdock, and even though he seemed small during class, come recess he would stretch out his neck and race around the classroom, making all kinds of strange noises.

Crow's father worked in the offices of the South Manchuria Railway Company, and the family lived in the center of town near the company. In Dalian, which was established by Russians during the age of imperial rule, the streets were neatly lined with houses topped by the chimneys from stoves and *pechka* cooking ovens that also provided heat for the homes. In the town square and along the wide streets that bore the names of the generals who had won victories in the Russo-Japanese War, rows of giant acacia and tall poplar trees stood at attention.

Old Manchurian men set down bird cages in the dense shade of these acacia trees and sipped their tea while they listened intently to the birds chirping. Coolies finished for a time with their labors took naps beneath these trees or chewed on Chinese dates, garlic, or steamed buns. After school, often Crow would not go straight home but would crouch down beside these old men and coolies, staring with hungry eyes at what the men were eating.

One autumn evening, Crow and three or four of his friends climbed to the roof of a house with a chimney, shouting boisterously as they gazed at the sky. Crow's younger sister, who was six years old, yelled from the garden, "Hey! What are you doing?" One of the boys answered, "We're up here looking at old men. Girls, go away!" Two days earlier, Crow had made a telescope out of rolled-up paper and peered into the sky as the sun was setting. In the quiet twilight, when Crow's mother took his sister to shop for food for their dinner, not a sound could be heard from any of the houses or gardens, not even those of the Russians next door. Just then, Crow suddenly spotted the face of an old man with a long beard in the gray, cloudy sky above the roof. It was the face of a man he had never seen or ever met.

Crow talked about his experience when he went to school. As he told the story over and over, he added that the old man had been chanting a spell: "YSSUPPUDEIRDADEKCILI!" Before long, even he almost began to believe that is exactly what the old man said.

And so that day, his friends came to his house to see the old man's face. But even after the sun set and it started to get cold, they saw nothing in the darkened sky, and they all began to grumble and call Crow a liar.

"Dang it!" When they had all gone home, Crow shook his head and took a stumpy piece of chalk out of his pocket, and on the fence of the Russians' house next door, where slivers of light from the setting sun still lingered faintly, he scribbled, "YSSUPPUDEIRDADEKCILI!" "I really did see that old man!" he mumbled. He was proud that his friends had not been able to guess the meaning of the spell. So he added, somewhat regretfully: "READ IT BACKWARDS!"

When the Japanese in Dalian talked about Japan, they called it "back home." Crow had been born and raised in Dalian, so he didn't know anything about "back home." So he, like the other children, only knew about "back home" from what his parents talked about, or by freely imagining what it looked like from the drawings in the children's magazines that arrived in Dalian two weeks after they went on sale in Japan. The scenes of Japan that Crow invented in his mind were of green hills off in the distance and of mothers with their heads wrapped in towels, resting along with their small children, probably around noontime, from their work in the tea fields. The mothers smiled at the young girls holding tea kettles. Crow found these silly color drawings in the children's magazines, and somehow came to the conclusion that this was "back home." Then he taped these pictures on the wall behind his study desk and sat with his chin in his hands, staring at them almost hypnotized; if his sister tried to touch any of them, he pouted his lips and scolded her. Crow had never seen these landscapes before. The scenes of nature that he was familiar with had sorghum fields, their plants twice as tall as he was, that stretched as far as the eye could see, along with other scenes from the Chinese continent where the sun when it set above the fields was as red as ripe apricots.

But come May, even in Dalian the poplars put out green

leaves and flowers bloomed on the willows and acacia trees. The warm winds sent countless downy catkins adrift over the sidewalk; they coiled around the shoulders of passersby and were tossed as high as the rooftops. Beneath the white acacia flowers, drivers of horse-drawn coaches cracked their whips, and mules stamped their hooves while the flower petals scattered on their backs and onto the laps of the drivers.

Before long, the sultry summer winds from the continent began to blow. A quiet swept over the Japanese village and the neighborhoods of the Manchurians; sometimes the guttural cries of Eurasian magpies could be heard from the grove inside West Park; and the coolies slept like the dead in the black blotches of shade: that was summer in Dalian. Yet at the beginning of October a cold wind blew away the acacia leaves, the whole town shivered a leaden color, and the people began to prepare for a cold winter and its snows.

When Crow turned nine, another dark, late autumn came to Dalian. Around that time, his parents suddenly began secluding themselves in the parlor until late into the night, where they seemed to be having some kind of conversation. They had begun discussing a divorce. From his room Crow could see the lights on in the parlor until deep into the night. Lying on a futon beside his sleeping sister, he lifted his dusky face and stared with goggly eyes at those lights. Sometimes he could hear his father's sharp voice and his mother's sobs. Crow wiped his nose with the sleeve of his nightshirt, burrowed down into his futon, and stuffed his fingers into his ears. Near midnight, when his parents had stopped fighting and walked past their children's room, his teary-eyed mother peered at her son with his face buried in his futon, while behind her, his father stood with folded arms and an ill-tempered look on his face.

"Plugging up his ears like this . . . Oh, it's so sad! It's just too sad! Making our children do something like this . . . ? Doesn't your conscience bother you in the least when you look at him?"

"Idiot. Don't be talking like that in front of the children."

Crow opened his eyes just a crack and peeked at his mother and father, pretending to be asleep.

After this, Crow began to tell lots more of his wild tales at school. During break time between classes, he would roam around the classroom and tell his classmates stories: that he had found a dog at a house near the Dalian Shrine that said "Hi!" instead of "Woof!"; or that he had discovered a sparkling chunk of ore in West Park that might be gold. During class time, instead of listening to what his teachers were saying, ridiculous stories would pop into his head, one after another. On his way home from school, he would lead a group of classmates who had believed his stories, and they would wander aimlessly for one or two hours looking for that dog, or picking up stones one after another and then discarding them in West Park, while meanwhile, as the evening mist drifted in, Crow began to half believe that his lies might be true. One of the friends he had dragged here and there finally got tired and said, "I'm going home. It's gotten cold." To which Crow would respond, "Search just a little longer, please. I think this time we're really going to find something."

* * *

To tell the truth, Crow wanted to delay his return home by even just a little. Around this hour his mother would be sitting motionless as a fossil in the darkened house, lost in thought. In the past, she would scold him if he romped around in the yard or in his room instead of doing his homework, but now, even as the waning sun gradually crept away from their yard, she still sat in the parlor without saying a word.

So when his friends abandoned him and returned to their homes, he would continue walking, keeping his distance from the road leading to his home. As usual, he would take a stubby piece of chalk and scribble "YSSUPPUDEIRDADEKCILI!" on fences, or on a road strewn with fallen acacia leaves he would stare at the old Russian man who sold clumsily drawn religious art or cheap medallions. This old man appeared near Crow's house every afternoon. No more than two or three Manchurians and two or three Japanese children would gather round the old man, his eyelids red and a brown cap on his head.

"And always, always Christ is . . ." The old man loudly blew his nose into a dirty handkerchief and wiped the sleep from his eyes. "Christ is always with you. He plays along with you. He knows the times you are cold, and the times when you are sad."

When he finished talking, the wind scattered the dry leaves. Suddenly the old man's expression turned mean as he tried to pawn off his medallions and miniature paintings to the assembled few. Refusing, the Manchurians waved their hands with a mocking smile, and the Japanese children jeered at him with singsong voices. Crow ran a little distance away, then stopped. When the old man flushed a bright red and shook his fist at the boy, Crow shouted "Amen! Ramen!" and fled.

* * *

"Tsutomu, let's go look at the ships!" One Sunday afternoon, Crow's father unexpectedly invited him on an outing.

Crow looked up at his father with fright in his eyes and stole a glance at his mother, who was behind him. His mother was wiping the table, her face stiff, and said nothing.

"We're going to go see the ships, Tsutomu."

Crow had caught a cold four days earlier, and he stuck his fingers into the stained dressing that was wrapped around his neck, the look on his face suggesting he was swallowing a bitter potion.

"What's wrong? Don't you want to go?"

"Yeah, I'll go." Crow nodded, his voice weak, and casting another quick glance at his mother, he stood up.

That Sunday afternoon, a swirling wind blew paper scraps and litter from the street corner into the gray sky. On a busy corner, the curtains on the street stalls flapped drily, and hawkers standing under pheasants and pig heads that dangled overhead called out to the Manchurians amid the smells of garlic and frying oil. Many Japanese families were also strolling along the narrow, crowded alleys. Crow looked at the Japanese children who peered into every stand to their right and left as their parents scolded them.

"Would you like me to buy you something?" Seeing those families, Crow's father placed his hand on his son's shoulder and, as if to gain Crow's favor he asked, "You once said you'd like a child's camera, didn't you? What was it called—a Tōgō camera?"

His father's hand on his shoulder felt very heavy to the boy. "Don't want one."

"Why not?"

"The school trip got cancelled . . . It's too late."

Crow was telling a lie. He was still thinking about his mother's rigid face as she silently wiped the table.

"Is that right?"

His father looked down at him with sad eyes and he ran his fingers through his hair, then suddenly set off with long strides, as though to shake off his disappointment.

The wind was blowing and it was cold at the wharf. Light was shining from a distant lighthouse, and waves glazed with oil lapped gently against the pier. Coolies passed them by, carrying bags of cement on their shoulders. Japan was far away on this dark sea.

"That ship's heading out." With both hands thrust into the pockets of his jacket, his lanky father was staring at a small cargo ship that was moving near the lighthouse. "I love ships. Wouldn't you like to ride on a ship?"

Crow shook his head.

"I love ships," his father muttered again, as though to himself as he watched the dark sea and the cargo ship. Then, wiping the dust from his trousers, he said, "Well then, let's go buy you a child's camera."

This time, when he saw his father's sad eyes, Crow couldn't refuse. Just as earlier, when he couldn't help but take in the image of his mother sitting fossil-like in the dark evening room. If he was going to have to hurt one or the other of his parents, Crow didn't know which he would choose. On their way back to the house, he had to quietly submit to having a black, box-shaped camera purchased for him at a Manchurian man's stall.

Even after they returned home, for some reason his father didn't tell anyone that he had bought a camera for Crow. Being the kind of child he was, Crow didn't show it either to his mother or to his younger sister. Father and son avoided each other's eyes as they stood in the entryway, like a parent and child who had been quarreling, and then headed off to their separate rooms. Crow hid the package containing the camera in his treasure chest along with youth magazines, a broken watch, and some stones he had picked up on a school outing.

"Where did you go with your father? Tell me, where did you go?" His mother, who came into his room shortly thereafter, caught hold of Crow and demanded an answer. "Did you meet anyone? Did your father really not meet anybody?"

He saw for the first time in his mother's fierce look a face that in no way resembled that of the mother he had known up until then. He saw the face of another woman, someone who was not his mother.

But no more than two or three days had passed before his mother found the camera. His sister had discovered it while he was away.

"Just what is this?"

His sister, looking half embarrassed and half pleased with herself, looked at Crow from behind their mother.

"I borrowed it."

"Why would you hide something you'd only borrowed?"

"Well . . . I—"

"Don't lie to me. Trying to win over a child by buying him something . . . Who does he think he's fooling?"

Crow's mother slapped him. The cheek she slapped stayed hot for some time, and with both hands pressed against his cheek he sat down in a corner of his room and cried. Evening came and the room turned dark, but he kept making weeping sounds even though he shed no more tears when, with catlike footsteps his sister stole in and crept up beside him. With inquisitive eyes but a fawning voice, she said, "Tsutomu, I'm sorry. C'mon, it's okay."

"You, and Mom . . . I hate all women," Crow shouted. "All you women!"

* * *

Winter came racing in to Dalian in October. Around this time, cold winds swept over the land, and the clattering of the hooves of horses as they dashed along the roads pulling carriages sounded all the more piercing. And it was at this time that Manchurian vendors wearing large gloves roasted Tianjin chestnuts in kettles to sell to passersby.

During this season, the children in Dalian would pick out large, strong-looking poplar leaves from those that had fallen to the ground and wage battles with their stems. They would tie the stem of their leaf with that of an opponent, and when they were yanked, the stem that was not cut was declared winner. The cunning boys would thread wires through the poplar stems. Not even the strongest of stems had any chance of beating those reinforced with wire.

Crow came up with various plans to strengthen the poplar leaf stems he had collected. He tried coating them with wax or boiling them in hot water. Finally, he announced to his friends that one day he had come up with a plan. He told them that after he had reinforced a poplar stem with his method, it would never lose to another boy's stem.

At recess his friends, shouting "Tsutomu, tell us!," gathered around Crow. He stretched out his neck to display his dark face and goggled his eyes with tremendous pride. He waved his hands and shouted "The secret! The secret!" He was very pleased to be the only one who knew this method.

But Crow had told just one friend what his secret method was. It was his close friend, Yokomizo. The secret plan that

Crow had devised was to bury the poplar leaves and then several times a day to pee on the ground where he had buried them. Yokomizo confided the method to another of his friends, who then passed it on to other boys. When finally their school teacher, Mr. Ōtsuka, heard about it, he told the entire class, "It's very impressive that Tsutomu came up with this idea on his own. But from the standpoint of hygiene it's a bad plan, so don't use it."

Crow blushed at being praised by his teacher, then scratched his head with embarrassment.

* * *

Crow's mother had recently begun frequenting the home of an elderly shamaness who lived in Nogimachi. The old woman prayed to the Fox God and inquired many things of this deity. His mother went to this house to have the old woman tell her about her husband.

Just once she took Crow with her to the shamaness's home. The house was permeated with the smell of old tatami and the toilet, and on the lintel hung a yellowing photograph (probably clipped out of the special edition of an old magazine) of the Emperor dressed in a military uniform, with the Empress beside him. With a smile the old woman stroked Crow's head and gave him a sticky senbei cracker. Then abruptly she seemed to fix her dark eyes on a spot in space and lit a candle on the kamidana shrine.

During her lengthy prayer, Crow stayed behind his mother and watched the old woman with fear in his eyes. As the woman's mouth mumbled something, she would sometimes move her clasped hands vigorously up and down.

"Madam, you must be careful! The god has said something terrible."

The old woman stared at Crow with a fearsome face. Unruffled, his mother asked, "Well then, what is it?"

"Your husband is determined to steal your son from you, just snatch him away. And this boy, I don't know, he's not reliable."

"Oh my, oh my!" His mother continued to play innocent. "What a disturbing divination!"

Still, on their way home his mother suddenly stopped in her tracks. Hugging Crow tightly, she said, "Tsutomu, you must never forget. You are your mother's son. You're on my side."

"Uh-huh," Crow nodded wearily. "I un-der-stand."

"You don't really understand."

"No, I . . . Leave me alone!"

Crow faked a yawn and gazed with a depressed look at the sky that spread out along the opposite side of the road. The sky was heavy and overcast. Starting now, three cold days would be followed by four warm days, the precursor of winter in Dalian. For some reason, Crow wanted to leave behind his sister and father and mother and keep walking endlessly along this gray road toward this cloudy sky.

The first snows fell at the end of October. Carrying metal poles wrapped in rags, coolies came to the Japanese village to clean out the *pechka* chimneys. Maids brought coal from sheds to the main houses. Black powder from the charcoal dotted the snow that had fallen in a single night. Crow collected enough snow to build a snowman, but since he didn't have any charcoal like the children "back home," he used tiny pieces of coal to make the eyes and mouth.

"Tsutomu, your snowman's face is all crooked," said his sister, who wore rubber boots and was warming her hands with her breath. "But it looks like Jesus."

"Why?"

"I saw him once when I went to Sunday School."

Crow remembered the face of the old Russian. He had placed poorly painted religious images and medallions on the sidewalk to sell. Whenever the children teased him, he would turn bright red and shake his fist at them. But now that his sister mentioned it, the face of Crow's snowman did look like the picture of Jesus in the religious paintings the old man was selling.

Several slightly warmer days followed the first snows. The continental pattern of three cold days, then four days warm, began, followed by a severe winter with temperatures fifteen and even five degrees. The smoke from the *pechka* ovens gradually shrank the snowman and turned it an ugly black.

One Sunday afternoon, their father invited Crow and his sister to go for a walk with him. Crow was somewhat relieved that his sister was joining them so that it wasn't only him this time. But just as on that earlier day, he glanced at his wordless mother's stiff face as he put on his overcoat.

"Tsutomu." When his father went to the entryway, she quietly called her son. "Don't go wandering off. You stay with your father wherever he goes. No matter what your father says to you."

A store selling lovely Russian candies stood where the great square at the center of the town intersected with Naniwa-machi, the busiest shopping area. Japanese and Russian families sipped tea at samovars and ate sweets filled with dried grapes. Crow sat down with his father and sister next to a stove that burned brightly red. When he spooned some ice cream in his mouth, Crow thought of his mother sitting all alone in their house.

"Say, aren't you going to finish eating that?"

"I've had enough of this."

With a look of annoyance, his father said, "Tsutomu, it's naughty of you to not eat it when you had me order it for you. If that's how you're going to be, Sachi, you eat what your brother's left. I just don't know how to deal with a selfish child like your brother."

With a quick sideward glance at Crow, she nonchalantly slid his bowl of ice cream toward her place.

"Anyway, anyway . . ." Their father suddenly looked up with bloodshot eyes at the clock on the wall and ran his fingers through his hair as though in a great hurry. "Father has got to get to work. You two go straight home when you're done."

The promise he had made to his mother when he left the house weighed heavily on Crow's heart. If her two children returned home alone, no doubt she would form a dark, pained furrow between her brows and sit back silent as a fossil. It was heartbreaking for Crow to see her like that.

"Is something wrong? You can go home, just the two of you, can't you?"

With the tip of his shoe, Crow traced the white liquid from the ice cream that had dropped to the floor and said nothing.

"All right, all right," their father said in a suddenly gentle voice. "Don't worry. I'll go home with you."

When they went outside, the air was chilly, and the lingering snow on the withered grasses at the town square glittered blue, while the mules of the waiting carriages hung their heads, shivering. Greatly relieved, Crow began to sing from an excess of happiness:

"Chinchin, chinapoi, chinchikurin no chikuchiku, paipu!"[1]

"What's that song?"

"It's really popular at school right now. Everybody is singing it, Father. The next words are 'chinaya, nichipaipu.' It's funny, isn't it?"

"I guess. In any case, Tsutomu . . ." As they walked along, his father sighed deeply. "To tell you the truth . . ."

Crow stared as his father's expelled breath blew whitely through the cold air.

"To tell you the truth, your mother may have to go back to Japan to take care of some things." The father and his two children continued to walk in silence, each breathing whitely.

"Father will be staying here in Dalian. And so . . ." He tried to sound cheerful, but his voice rang false. "Since Sachi is a girl, let's say she goes back home with her mother . . . and Tsutomu, will you live here with me?"

A single leaf still clung to its branch on an acacia tree on the opposite side of the road. It clung there. Clung there. *Why are they doing this to me? They annoy me and lie to me,* Crow thought.

* * *

"Why can't Sachi stay here too?" Crow actually wanted to ask why his mother couldn't stay in Dalian, too. But he substituted his sister's name to avoid embarrassing his father.

1. The words of this children's song appear to be meaningless despite various attempts to parse them.

His father realized what his son was doing, but said, "Sachi is still young, and she'd be sad if she wasn't with her mother. Wouldn't you, Sachi?"

"I'd like to be with Mom."

Sachi nodded and took her father's hand as though to fawn on him. Crow didn't blame his sister; rather he felt it was cunning of his father to pretend to not know what she was doing.

"Besides, Tsutomu, you'll soon be in middle school, and it would be a shame for your grades to drop just because you changed schools. Don't you think it'd be best to stay with your father? . . . Anyway, think about it."

That night, the lights in the parlor stayed on endlessly, and for the first time in a while the children could hear their father's sharp voice and their mother's weeping. Crow stuck his fingers in his ears.

* * *

A thief who was after coal was apprehended in a shed in the Japanese district. He was a Manchurian about forty years old. Word was that he had been stuffing coal into a sack when a woman who innocently opened the door to the shed discovered him. She pushed the door shut with her large behind and yelled for help, pressing with both hands against the fence that lay opposite the shed.

Several Japanese and Manchurians had gathered by the shed before the police arrived. Of course Crow was also one who ran at full speed to the house. He poked his face, dark as a great bullock, in front of everyone else and watched with eager excitement as the police bound the thief with ropes. The Manchurian was tall and had a beard, and he was clearly a man of great strength, but he stood straight as a rod and gave no resistance.

The thief was led to the police station near the Dalian Shrine. The children made a racket as they followed behind, keeping a safe distance. They stood on tiptoes to peer through the window at the back of the station and watched as two Japanese policemen took turns beating and kicking the Manchurian prisoner in a small tatami room. While one was beating the man, the other took a break, warming his hands over a hibachi stove. Crow suddenly became frightened and returned home.

His mother was standing distractedly at the doorway.

"Mother!" Crow panted, "A thief broke in at the Ōtsuka's house!"

"I don't care." Her face was ferocious. "Follow your father, he just slipped out of the house. You find out who he's seeing and come tell me."

She wrapped a scarf around his neck and all but shoved him outside the gate. It was odd that he did not encounter a single person on the gray road that ran between his house and the public square. But when that road ended, Crow caught sight on a slope in the distance the tiny figure of his father, hurrying along without a coat and with both hands thrust into his pants pockets. Chewing on the scarf, Crow followed.

"Young man. Would you like a ride?" An empty carriage stopped behind him and the driver called out. In that moment, Crow lost sight of his father. Just a moment earlier, a pale sun had lit up the slope where his father had been, but all he could see in that sunlit spot now were the figures of four coolies crouched down smoking.

"Tsutomu!" Crow unexpectedly heard his father's voice call from behind him. "What are you doing?"

Crow had no answer.

"Did your mother tell you to follow me? . . . I see." His father stared at him, at a loss what to say. "Now what should I do?"

Crow buried his face in the scarf that was damp with spittle and sighed. He felt more like crying than his father did.

"Tsutomu, your mother and I are getting a divorce. I know you don't understand yet what that means, but things just aren't working out. So how about you live with your father?"

"But why?!" Crow flushed red in an effort to hold back the tears. "Why? Why! I . . . I can't stand this!"

"That's what I'm trying to explain to you," his father shouted, flustered. "Your father has to help you become a fine young man. I have to repay you for all the trouble I'm causing you. I want to take care of you, even if your mother ends up caring for Sachi."

Crow stared fixedly as his father's lips repeatedly opened and closed. For the first time in his life, he detected a lie told by someone other than himself. He didn't know the reason, but he felt that his father's lie was sadder and more pitiful than his own. The two faced one another on that twilight slope. Father and son faced each other in the cold Dalian air as though they had been standing there for hundreds of years.

"No, that's not it. Your father . . ." His father's eyes darkened like those of some animal. "Your father is lonely. And it's cold. I want to have you with me."

Ah, this too was a lie. But the word "cold" stabbed at

Crow's greatest weakness. These eyes staring at him were not those of his father but of a pleading adult, and they rattled and tore Crow apart.

"Will you stay with me?"

"Umm." A tiny sound that was either a sigh or a voice of assent emerged from the depths of Crow's scarf. It was the voice of him betraying his mother.

After his father went into the house, Crow stood motionless outside the doorway. Before long his mother would hear what he had promised his father. Again that night, the lights would stay on in the parlor, and well into the night he would hear the weeping of his mother, who would learn of his betrayal. Crow had betrayed his mother.

"YSSUPPUDEIRDADEKCILI!"

Crow rubbed his hands together, stripped off his overcoat and undid the buttons on his pants. Then, in the shade of the fence, he peed on the yet unmelted snow. Sprinkled with his urine, the snow was stained a yellow not unlike the color of the lemon ices he would eat during summer vacation. In the darkened garden, the shrunken snowman had tumbled over into an ugly pile. His sister had called the snowman "Jesus." Crow remembered the words muttered at the streetcorner by the old Russian man as he wiped his nose and eyes with a filthy handkerchief: "And always, always Christ is with you. He plays along with you. He knows the times you are cold, and the times when you are sad."

What the hell! How could he know? How could he know? Crow kicked the snowman with his boot. In despair, over and over he had written on the cold fences with chalk, shouting "Read it backwards! Read it backwards!": YSSUPPUDEIRDADEKCILI!

And that's how the story goes.

Shadows

I don't know whether I'll actually send this letter. I've already written you something like three letters. But I've either broken them off halfway, or, if I've been able to finish them, I've stuck them in my desk drawer and never mailed them to you.

Each time I've tried writing to you, I found myself wondering if in fact the letter is not meant for you but addressed to myself, to calm my anxieties and bring some degree of understanding to my mind. Ultimately the reason I never sent any of the letters I wrote is probably because I felt the act of writing was pointless, and brought no satisfaction to the depths of my heart. But circumstances are somewhat different now. I feel now that a gradual understanding, though imperfect, is budding in my mind with regard to what you did.

Where can I begin? Should I start with my recollections of meeting you in my childhood, when you first arrived in Japan? Or should I begin with the day my mother died, when you opened the front door for me after I raced home, only to shake your head and say, "She's gone."

As a matter of fact, I ran into you yesterday. You of course had no idea that I was there, or that you were being watched. As you sat at the table waiting for your food to be brought, you pulled a book from your old black bag (I remember that bag) and began reading. That reminded me of the way, when you were a priest, you would take out your breviary before meals and open it up. We were at a small restaurant in Shibuya, and the pedestrians walking in the drizzling rain outside the clouded window looked like fish in an aquarium. I sat with the sports page of the newspaper spread out, shoveling curry rice into my mouth with one hand. The news that one of my favorite players in the Taiyō team was going to be traded was announced in large lettering. At the bottom of the page, a novel by a friend of mine was being serialized.

When I glanced up, a foreigner dressed in black with his back toward me was about to sit down in a corner of the restaurant. I was startled. I hadn't seen you in six years. Our seats were separated by some twenty meters, while between us four or five businessmen at the same table were eating hamburger steaks.

". . . The gears in that car are hard to operate, aren't they?"

"I don't think so. . . ."

Those fragments of conversation reached my ears. One of them had a dark-red blemish the size of a ten-yen coin on his balding forehead.

You gave an affable smile to the young waitress who brought you a glass of water, then pointed to something on the menu. The waitress nodded and left, and then you pulled an English book out of your old black bag and began reading. Actually, I don't know if it was in English, but it was written in horizontal lines. He's got really old, I thought. He's a decrepit old man. To say this is to run the risk of offending a man who had served as a missionary, but in your youthful days you were truly a handsome rogue. I can still remember that when I first met you in the Kobe hospital and saw your deep-etched face and your wine-colored eyes, even as a child I thought what a splendid man you were. Now that face has been eroded by age, your chestnut hair has thinned (my own, I admit, is rather sparse), and your cheeks just below your eyes are red and puffy, as though celluloid bags had been implanted there. In that face I tried to sniff out the loneliness that has been yours since the incident. I tried to ascertain your struggles since you took on the burdens of a wife and children and had to find a job in a foreign land, and the pain you've had to endure after losing your friends and anyone who might help you.

I wanted to stand up and walk over to you and say: "Hello, it's been a long time!" But I remained in my chair, unable to speak to you, and like a detective in an investigation bureau, I hid my face behind the newspaper and scrutinized you. Certainly curiosity was at work. And my interest in human behavior as a novelist played a part, too. But there was more to it. Some powerful force in my mind held me back and prevented me from coming over to you. I'm planning to write about the power that restrained me in this letter. In any case, I sat there spying on you. Finally the waitress brought you a plate full of food. You nodded and smiled as you had before, then tucked a handkerchief into your shirt in place of a napkin. I was still watching you intently. You straightened your chair and sat up squarely in it. And then you brought your fingers up to your chest, and quickly, so that no one would notice, you crossed yourself. An inexpressible emotion surged through me at that moment. "So, you're still like that, after all?"

The force that stopped me from going to your table—it's

hard to explain what it was. Because, to put it in different terms, it's one of the major rivers that have given shape to my life. I've written a number of different novels over the years by thrusting my hands into those rivers. I've plucked up objects that have been deposited at the bottom of my river, washed the dirt from them, and arranged them all together. There are many important objects there that I still haven't dredged up. I haven't yet written anything about my father, whom you never met, or my mother, whom you looked after in so many ways throughout her life. Nor have I yet turned my hand to a depiction of you. No, that's not true. Since I first became a novelist, I've changed various details about your life and written about you on three different occasions. Over the many years since that incident, you have been an important narrative figure for me. Even though you're such a crucial character, virtually every story I've written about you has been a failure. I know why. It's because I still didn't have a firm grasp of who you are. Yet, though the failures continued to mount, you never ceased to hover around the world of my mind. How comfortable things would have been for me if I'd been able to chase you out. But how could I possibly drive away my mother and you?

Whenever I look back along the river of my life, somehow I always think of that little church in the Hanshin district where I was compelled to receive baptism. That tiny little Catholic church, it remains unchanged even today. The pseudo-Gothic steeple, the gold cross, the oleanders in the garden. As you know, my mother had separated from my father because of her tempestuous personality, and she took me back to Japan from Dalian in Manchuria, and we moved in with her elder sister in Hanshin. This sister was a devout

Christian, and at her encouragement Mother began to seek healing of her desolate heart through faith. Of necessity I began attending the church, escorted there by my mother and aunt. A French priest was in charge of the church. As the war grew more fierce, one day this priest from the Pyrenees was hauled off by two military policemen who had stormed into the church. He was suspected of being a spy.

But all that happened much later. The war had already started in China, but times had not yet become that difficult for the Catholic Church in Japan. At Christmas they could still ring out the hallelujah bells in the depths of the night, and on Easter Sunday flowers adorned the gates and doors of the church, and we beamed with pride while mischievous boys from the neighborhood looked on enviously at the young girls decked out in white veils like those the foreign girls wear. One Easter day, the French priest lined up ten children and asked each of them: "Do you believe in Christ?" And each of them parroted back: "I believe." I was one of those children. Imitating the voices of the other children, I loudly called out: "Yes, I believe."

During the summer holiday, one of the seminarians at the church often performed stories for us with illustrations drawn on paper. He also took us hiking up Mt. Rokkō. After he returned to his home, we boys would frequently play catch in the garden of the church. Once when someone missed the ball it struck a window, and the French priest thrust his enraged face through the window and screamed at us. Not every day was a happy one for me, because my mother, separated from Father, would often sit with a dark expression on her face as she discussed something or other with my aunt. But unlike the time we were living in Dalian, I was spared the torment of suffering alone while my parents fought, and I think it was a relatively stable period for me.

Once in a while an old foreigner would come to the church. He would pick a time when none of the members were there, but while we were playing baseball we saw him sneaking into the priest's quarters. "Who is that?" I asked my aunt and mother, but for some reason they averted their eyes and said nothing. But one of my friends told me about the man, who dragged one of his legs as he walked. "He was kicked out." Although he had been a priest, he had married a Japanese woman; because he had been expelled from the Church, none of the members would ever say a word about him, and they clamped their mouths shut, as though the very mention of his name would sully their faith. The only person who would meet him was the priest from the Pyrenees. As for me, I stole glances at the old man with feelings that combined fear with curiosity and a certain enjoyment. Having spent my childhood in Dalian, in that emigrant colony I had seen several old White Russians who had been driven from their homeland, and the face of one of those old men who had come to the Japanese settlement selling Russian bread reminded me of this man. Both of them wore overcoats that gave the impression less that they were worn than that they were demolished; around their necks both wore large, hand-knitted scarves, and they both dragged their rheumatic legs and stopped from time to time to wipe their noses with large, filthy handkerchiefs. Thinking back on them now, I realize that the lonely shadows clouding their faces were similarly imbued with the pain of those who have been exiled from the thing that has sustained the very core of their lives.

It was an evening during the summer holiday. I was walking along a road. I suppose I must have been on my way to play baseball. In front of the gate to the church, brightly illuminated by the twilight sun, I nearly ran smack into the old man. It never occurred to me that he might come out from the church. In surprise, I stood frozen, my body stiffened like a rock. The old man said something to me, but I had no idea what it was. I was filled with feelings of revulsion and fear. I shook my head and made a quick attempt to race up the stone steps leading to the chapel. But a large hand gripped my shoulder. "Not to worry," or "Nothing to be scared"—the old man said something of the kind to me in broken Japanese. His breath was foul. In desperation I fled. All I could remember was the sad look in his wine-colored eyes as he gazed at me then. When I got home I told my mother what had happened, but she said nothing. After two or three days, I too had forgotten all about it.

Strangely enough, only a month after this incident occurred you came into my life. I can't help but feel now that this coincidence has had great meaning in the river of my life. A year ago, as I was composing a long novel, I frequently pondered that coincidence. In the novel, I had my protagonist compare the weary, haggard, worn and sunken face of Christ in the *fumie* with the face of Christ that appears in Western devotional painting—the face filled with tranquility, purity, and fervor. As I composed those scenes, the images that surfaced in my mind were of your face from then, and the face of that outcast old man.

The autumn of that same year, I developed appendicitis and had to enter the Charity Hospital at Nada. After my stitches were removed, my aunt and mother were feeding me rice gruel when you suddenly came into my hospital room. The two women stood up in surprise. They were not taken aback because a priest had come in. The only priests we had ever seen, whether the priest at our church or any other father, had all been scrawny men wearing thick spectacles. The Japanese fathers in particular always looked so peculiar we couldn't decide whether they were Japanese or Nisei. When you opened that door and came in the room, you were completely different from the others. With your solid body clothed in a well-kept black suit with a pure white Roman collar and a gentlemanly smile on your well-nourished face, you were enough to throw the three of us Japanese into a state of confusion. After giving a polite greeting to my aunt and mother, you looked down at me. I lay there stiff as a rock, still clutching my chopsticks and rice-bowl in my hands. Your Japanese was very fluent. Sweat beaded my forehead as I tried earnestly to answer your questions. "Yes, I'm well now." "No, I'm not lonely." After you left, I cried out "What a handsome man!" and my mother heaved a deep sigh. "What a pity that a man like that became a priest and can't get married." My aunt chided my mother for her impious remark.

But it seems that my mother did take a great deal of interest in you. When she came to visit my room, without fail she would ask whether you had been in to see me.

"You're such a bother. For God's sake leave me alone!" Feeling somehow ill at ease, I was intentionally rude to her. But out of feminine curiosity my mother learned that you had been a soldier who graduated from the military academy in Spain, that you'd had a change of heart and abandoned the military in order to follow the path of a priest, that you had gone to seminary, and that after coming to Japan you had spent a year at a monastery in Kakogawa.

"He's not like your ordinary priests. He was born into a scholar's family. I can imagine how truly happy it must make his mother to have a splendid son like him."

Mother said this to encourage me, but even as a child I could sense that these were not words directed exclusively at her son.

Even after I was released, Mother frequently brought me to the hospital. She was not satisfied with what the run-of-the-mill priests had to say. Though she had in fact been baptized, with her stern character she must have felt that something she starved for had been satisfied when you suddenly appeared in front of her. My father, who was cautious and preferred to tread the asphalt highway of a circumspect life, had been unable to bear the way my mother lived. Christianity, to which my mother had drawn near at her sister's encouragement to assuage her temporary solitude, began at this point in time to become something true to her. Besides teaching music at several schools in the Hanshin region, she began devouring the books that you lent her one after another. And from that time her life changed completely. She demanded of herself a strict life of prayer, like a nun's existence, and required the same of me. Each morning she took me to Mass, and in every free moment she recited her rosary. She even seemed to have started thinking about bringing me up to become a priest like you.

I have no intention of writing about the spiritual association between you and my mother. But two years later, you began visiting our home every Saturday as my aunt's and my mother's guidance priest. Friends of my aunt and members of the church also assembled there. I can admit this to you now: the days when you came over were very painful for me. Mother became even more stern than usual, and made me wash my hands and get my hair cut, and she gave me strict orders, saying: "Now you behave yourself properly when Father comes over." Even worse, how was I supposed to understand anything you said there amongst the adults? Whether because I was nervous, or because I was prone to tiredness (you are well aware of how physically weak I've been from childhood), it took all my energy to fight off drowsiness as I sat beside my mother. Who cares anything about the Old Testament or the New Testament or Christ or Moses? I did everything I could think of—pinching my knees, thinking about something else—to fight the boredom and my increasingly heavy eyelids. My mother glared at me with fearsome eyes. I was able to stay awake for the full hour from dread of that gaze.

On summer mornings without fail, and even on wintry mornings, my mother never allowed me to miss going to church. 5:30 a.m. While darkness still clung to most of the sky and every house was fast asleep, I would walk behind her as she silently prayed, blowing on my hands to warm them as we made our way along the frost-frozen road to the church. Beside the feeble candle at the altar the French priest hunched over, his hands clasped, and recited the Mass, his shadow etched against the wall. The only people kneeling within the frigid chapel were two old women, my mother and I. When I nodded off as I pretended to pray, Mother would glare at me with a frightening face.

"Do you think you can become like the Father if you behave like that?"

"The Father," of course, was you. To her you had become the idealized image of my future, the portrait of the man I was impelled to become. Of necessity I developed a revulsion toward you, and I grew sick of your immaculate clothes, your well-cared-for face and fingers. I could no longer stand your proud smile, your learning, or your faith. Do you remember that it was around this time my grades at school began to drop? I was in my second year of middle school, but I consciously set out to become a lazy, slovenly boy. Because a lazy, slovenly person was indisputably the opposite of what you were. In rebellion against my mother for trying to fashion me into a man like you who lived with profound conviction and confidence in your faith and your way of life, I purposely went out of my way to neglect my studies and become as poor a student as I could. When Mother was around I made as though I was busy at my study desk, but I did absolutely nothing.

I had a dog then. He was a mongrel I got from the eel-shop owner in our neighborhood. Without any siblings, and having no friends with whom I could share my sorrow over the complicated rift between my parents, I showered affection on this dim-witted dog. Dogs and little birds still appear frequently in my fiction, but they are no mere decorations. In those days the only one I felt really understood my inexpressible loneliness was this mongrel. Even today, the moist, grieving eyes of dogs somehow remind me of the eyes of Christ. This Christ I speak of is, of course, not the Christ filled with assurance of his own way of life, as you once were. It is the weary Christ of the *fumie,* trampled upon by men and looking up at them from beneath their feet.

As was her habit, my mother began to berate me for the

decline in my grades. Evidently she sought counsel from you about this. With a faintly stern expression, you cautioned me to study diligently so that my mother would not worry. Inside my heart I muttered: "What the hell do you know? You're just a stupid foreigner." I set myself to become even more idle precisely because you were the one who admonished me to do better. One day you apparently told my aunt and my mother that in Western households children are punished a bit more frequently, that appropriate discipline is meted out to children who fail to make appropriate effort. And to punish me when my grades remained at the same low level during the third term, you ordered my mother to get rid of my dog.

I can still vividly remember my anguish then. Naturally I lent no ear to her orders. But one day when I returned home from school, my beloved pet was gone. She had got some boy in the neighborhood to drag him away. I'm sure you don't even remember this. To you the dog was nothing more than a deterrent from my studies, and I'm sure you felt that getting rid of the dog was for my own good. Of course I do not resent you for that. But one reason I bring up such trifling matters here is because they seem so typical of you. More than anything else, you hated weakness, laziness, and sloppiness in yourself and in others. I imagine it's because that's how your family was. Or perhaps your training as a soldier made you like that. "A man must be strong. He must constantly strive. He must steel himself in his life and in his beliefs." You never said as much in words, but you practiced these principles in your life. Everyone knows how energetically you threw yourself into your proselytizing work, how unflaggingly you studied theology. There is no room for criticism. Everyone (my mother included) looked up to you as a splendid human being. In my own childish way, I was the only one who began to suffer because of your unassailable goodness.

Unfortunately for me, you took on a new responsibility around that time. A dormitory for Christian students was erected on a hill at Mikage, and you were relieved of your duties as full-time priest at the Charity Hospital so that you could become the resident priest at this dormitory. "I'm really not cut out for this kind of job," you explained with a perplexed look to the people who had gathered for their regular instruction in the Bible. "But I have to do it, since the orders came from above." In spite of your denials, you seemed to be interested in the job. On our way home my mother suddenly asked me if I would like to move into your dormitory. She felt that, if I just lived beside you, my plummeting grades would return to their previous level, and that I would also grow in faith. I told her again and again that I didn't want to, but you remember how strong-willed she was. When I came home later that year with yet another disgraceful report card, I was placed in the dormitory where you had already been serving as dorm master for six months.

It was an austere lodging. I suppose you must have taken a Western seminary dormitory or a military academy barracks as your model. I'm not trying to make any excuses, but I really did make some effort. Yet everything turned out just the opposite of what you had hoped for me. I couldn't accept that the things you considered "for my own good" were really so. Even things I did with no ill intentions whatsoever you viewed as signs of my weakness. You tried to steel me, to hammer me into shape "for Mother's benefit." You never realized that the hammer might eventually crush me.

There would be no end to it were I to begin writing down

each of those episodes. Do you remember when this happened? The dorm students (most of whom were college students; only I and another fellow, N, were still in middle school) would get up every morning at six and go to Mass, after which one of our daily duties was to jog along the mountain path behind the dorm to breakfast. I couldn't bear that. I'm sure it was nothing to you, after your military training, or to the college students at the dorm. But having weak bronchial tubes since childhood, I would be panting for breath in no time, and my eyes would begin to swim. After the run, greasy sweat painted my forehead, and I had lost all appetite for food, and sometimes I even felt light-headed. I came up with clever ways of avoiding running. But you finally found me out. You told me there was no reason why I shouldn't be doing exactly the same thing that the other middle-school boy, N, was doing. But with your robust physique, you could not understand how hard it was for someone physically weak like me to participate in that kind of training. "Everyone is running to build up their bodies. You're just not making the effort." That was your side of the story. To you I appeared to be a selfish boy with a dislike for group training.

Then we'd head off to our various schools, and when we returned, after dinner you lectured to us. I often dropped off to sleep. I dozed during evening prayers in the chapel afterward. With my frail constitution I got pretty worn out from the classes and military drill at school during the day, so I could get nothing out of an even more trying lecture on theology.

On one such evening, while everyone else was listening to your sermon, I was as always nodding off to sleep. Even though I was in the far back corner, I suppose I must have been snoring lightly too. You realized I had fallen asleep and you suddenly broke off your sermon. N, who was sitting beside me, poked me in the side, and I opened my eyes in surprise. To my embarrassment, I had drooled down my chin and soaked my jacket. At first everyone laughed, but when they noticed your stern look they suddenly turned silent. You unexpectedly raised one hand and shouted at me in Japanese: "Get out!"

That was the first time I saw you turn red and yell in anger. Normally you greeted my mother and aunt and the other believers with a gentlemanly smile, and this was the first time I saw your face twisted in rage. You were not angry with me for falling asleep. Later you explained to my mother that you had blown up at me because I was using my physical frailty as a general excuse for not conducting my life the way your dormitory students were expected to. That's certainly true. I admit that I didn't follow the daily routine at the dormitory whenever I could get out of it. I acknowledge that, as you claimed, I didn't try my hardest. But it's also a fact that I was physically unable to endure the kind of life you conceived as ideal. I'm not making excuses for the way I behaved then. All I'm trying to say is that your good intentions and determination, though they had positive results with those who were strong, for the weak were at times cruel, and instead of producing positive results simply inflicted unnecessary scars.

Finally, after less than ten months, I left your dormitory and returned to my mother's house. Still, being a mother, she struggled to discern some strong qualities or virtues in her useless son, but by then you seemed to feel nothing but disappointment and scorn for me. Your behavior toward me certainly didn't change from what it had been, but you began to speak to me less often. In this manner, my mother's dream—of making me into a priest like you—was shattered.

As I read over what I have written here, I fear that you may misunderstand me. I have in no way forgotten the kindness you extended to Mother and me. Far from it; I believe it was because of you that she was rescued from despair after her divorce, and because of you that she was able to immerse herself in the Christianity that sustained her spirit until her death. I always feel grateful to you for helping her in so many ways until she died.

What I'm trying to say is completely different. If there are the strong and the weak among human beings, in those days you were truly one of the strong. And I was a spineless weakling. You had confidence in your way of life, in your faith, in your body, and you performed your missionary work in Japan with firm conviction. In contrast, not once in my life have I been able to feel confidence and conviction about every facet of my life. As I say this, I imagine that in your current state you will understand everything. But in the past you would have resolutely shaken your head in disagreement. You would have shaken your head, and in a loud voice you would have cried that man exists so that he can strive to reach ever greater heights throughout his life. But weren't you forced to learn, some fifteen years later, that unexpected perils and danger spots like thin ice lurk within such strength, and that amidst such perils come the beginnings of true religion?

My mother died after I finished middle school and was entering into my second year in limbo, still unable to get into any higher school. I took one entrance exam and failed, then another and failed, until finally even Mother got tired of reprimanding me and would just heave deep sighs. When I remember that look on her face, even now it pains me to the heart. She began to tire easily and started to complain of occasional dizziness. When you took her to the hospital one day, the doctor found that her blood pressure was very high, but she refused to stop pushing herself, and she never missed morning Mass or relaxed her demanding way of life.

At the moment my mother died, I was seeing a film with a friend. I had deceived her by telling her that I was attending a college preparatory school, when in fact I was spending most of the day with friends at coffee shops and cinemas in Sannomiya. It was the end of December, and when I came out of the cinema it was pitch-black outside. I phoned home, planning to lie to Mother and tell her that we had been taking a practice test. To my surprise, the person who answered the phone was you. Mother had collapsed in the street, and you came rushing over as soon as you were notified. I learned for the first time that you had organized several groups of people to go out looking for me. When you asked "Where are you?" I quickly hung up the phone. How sluggish the Hankyū train taking me back home seemed! I had never raced home from the station so quickly. When I rang the bell, you were the one who opened the door for me. "She's gone" was all you muttered. Mother had been placed upon her bed; faint traces of agony were still lingering between her brows. My aunt and some people from the church had assembled there, and sensing their accusing eyes on me, I stared at Mother's waxy face. My mind was curiously clear, and in that moment I felt no pain or sorrow. I was merely at a loss. You said nothing to me. Only the others were able to weep.

When everyone went home after her funeral, my aunt

and you and I were left alone in the empty house. A decision had to be made about what to do with me. You were in more of a daze than I was. You seemed in a stupor, as though you had lost something that had previously been yours. So when my aunt asked me what I wanted to do, I told her that I didn't want to be a burden to anyone else. Then she suggested my father. Finally you lifted your bewildered face and expressed your view that everything should be handled according to my wishes. It was decided that you would explain the situation to my father.

I left the disposal of Mother's house to you and my aunt and returned to my father's home in Tokyo. From that day I began a life with a father and his new wife, toward neither of whom I could feel any affection as my parents.

After attempting to live with Father, I began to understand why Mother had left him. He was constantly saying things like "Mediocrity is the best way. The greatest happiness lies in not making waves." On days when he took a holiday from the company he managed, he would toy with his bonsai trees, tend the lawn in his yard, listen to a baseball game on the radio—that was his life. Every day he made some sort of effort to persuade me to choose the safe path of the businessman in my future. It was nothing like the rigorous daily life I had spent when there were only my mother and I. At her house, I was awakened each winter morning and walked down the frost-hardened path to the church. In the dark chapel where our only companions were the two elderly women, the French priest faced the cross, upon which Christ shed his blood. But in Father's house, not a word was ever said about life or religion, and the only topics of discussion were how noisy the neighbor's radio was, or how meager the rations of rice had become. Mother had tried to inculcate in me the belief that holy things were the most exalted and wonderful things upon the face of this earth. But the atmosphere at Father's suggested that any mention of such things would cause them to turn the other way, even to ridicule me. Living in what were considerably better material circumstances, I felt every single day that I was betraying Mother. It was painful, but not a day went by that I didn't think about the mother who now seemed very dear to me. The only things that served as meager compensation for the pangs of conscience I suffered were the letters I wrote to you. Because you had been the person Mother most respected up to the day of her death. By composing letters to you, I felt as though I were being saved, if even for a moment, from the self-reproach that came from knowing that I was in the process of betraying her wishes for me.

From time to time you would send a brief reply. Father snarled every time he saw an envelope addressed in your hand. I'm sure it must have bothered him to have memories of Mother still in his son's head, to have her words still lingering there, to have me feel close to her friends. Looking away from me, he muttered in annoyance: "You shouldn't associate with one of those useless 'Amen' priests." The following year, when I was somehow able to squeak my way into a private university, you notified me that you were taking up a position at a theology school in Tokyo.

* * *

It's the middle of the night. While my wife and child sleep, I sit up by myself in the house and resurrect each segment of my past so that I can write this letter. But as I read through what I have already written, I am amazed at the overwhelming number of incidents I haven't been able to write about. I realize even more emphatically now how difficult it is to talk about you, and to talk about my mother. In order to write down everything, I shall have to wait until the day comes when individuals will not be wounded by it—no, even more important, I shall have to write everything about myself. That is how inseparably tied my life is to you and Mother, how deeply the two of you have sunk your roots into me. Eventually, I suppose, I shall be able to describe in my own fiction the marks that you and Mother left upon me, and examine their essence.

But I must go back to where I left off if I am to continue this rough sketch. I went to see you as soon as you came to Tokyo. You hadn't changed at all. You didn't even have the pale complexion of other Fathers and seminarists. Your shoes were meticulously polished, the suit that encased your large body was carefully brushed and pressed, and you still spoke in the same confident manner. You were pleased that I had finally been accepted into college. "Do you believe in Christ? Are you still going to Mass?" When I said nothing, you looked displeased. "I know you're not too busy. Or are you using the old excuse that you're too physically weak?" Tinges of disappointment and contempt surfaced on your face, just as they had when I left your dormitory.

That elicited the same feelings of defiance I had experienced in my childhood. But, partly because you were very busy with your new job at the seminary, our meetings gradually became less and less frequent. Not that you ever ceased to exist within my mind. Even as I continued to live with my father, my attachment to Mother grew all the deeper, and the resentment I had once felt toward her was transformed into fond remembrance, and I even idealized her fervent personality. At the very least, she instilled into the very depths of my soul that even a laggard like me had to live on a higher plane of existence. And you, at the very least, constituted a major portion of what Mother was. I think I must have enrolled in the literature department at my college because I had observed the way she lived. It must have had something to do with my realization that the kind of life you and Mother led was a world apart from the lives of most people, including my father. The less my life was like yours, the more distant it became, the more frequently I would think of you and feel ashamed.

Ultimately the war drove an even broader wedge between us. One day I got an unexpected letter from you informing me that you had been forced to leave Tokyo and live in Karuizawa. You and the rest of the foreign priests had been compelled by the Japanese authorities to evacuate to Karuizawa. Although it was called "evacuation," clearly you lived a kind of concentration camp existence, being under constant watch of the Japanese MPs and police.

Around the same time, classes were cancelled at my school, and I was assigned to produce aircraft parts for Zero fighters while I cowered in fear of air raids at a plant in Kawasaki. It was no easy task even to buy a train ticket to Karuizawa. But one day, with a ticket finally in hand, I set out for that tiny village in Shinshū province. I still remember that when I got off the train the cold seemed sharp enough to slash my cheeks. This resort town, which must have been bustling in times of peace, was utterly desolate, darkly silent and gloomy. Two sharp-eyed men were warming themselves at a brazier in the MP office across from the station. A woeful plume of smoke rose from a grove of larch trees where some refugees were boiling a pot of rice porridge. I called at the office of the neighborhood association, and guided by the neighborhood chief I was able to find the large wooden Western-style building where you and your comrades were staying. We were reunited in the frozen garden. The chief stood a little apart from us, with his back turned, while you said: "You aren't skipping Mass, are you? You must believe in Christ." Even here your clothing, though thoroughly reduced to tatters, was carefully brushed. But your hands were swollen with frostbite. You went back into the building, and soon came out again with a package wrapped in newspaper.

"Take this back with you," you said quickly, placing the bundle in my hands. The chief noticed this and approached suspiciously. "What is that?" Angrily you replied: "It's my ration of butter. Is there anything wrong with giving him something that belongs to me?"

The war ended. You returned to Tokyo from Karuizawa, and I avoided the draft just before being snatched up and was able to go back to my broken-down college from the factory where I had been obliged to work. A new age dawned for Christianity in Japan. The priests like yourself, who had been forced to evacuate during the war under suspicion from the police that they were spies, began now to perform their missionary work with impunity, and some Japanese began to attend church in search of the power to live, while others came out of desire for food and material possessions, while yet others came to have contact with foreigners. I often saw you in those days driving out of the seminary at the wheel of a Jeep; you were very busy then. It was your responsibility to enlarge the seminary, which had been very small before. When I came to see you in your semicircular office, one of the rare Quonset huts around in those days, your secretary was busily handling the telephone calls that were coming in rapid succession. "I'm sorry, but the Father isn't in at the moment," she would often curtly reply. "I'm afraid I have no idea when he'll be able to see you."

None of this really matters. I write down such inane details because I hesitate to touch on what is really the central concern of my letter. I've now come to the stage where I must relate it, and I can sense the point of my brush dulling. The fear that I will wound you deeply has restrained me in what I have written thus far. Please forgive me.

But how should I phrase it? Exactly how did it happen? Even now I have no idea. I don't know how to interpret what gradually took place within your heart. Somerset Maugham has a novel called *Rain,* in which a clergyman bit by bit violates the restrictions on his behavior and begins to love a woman. Maugham attempts to explain that whole process from without, using the image of long, monotonous rain. As a literary technique it is superb, but I cannot bring myself to employ such manipulation when I think about what you did. After it happened, everyone was saying: "I can't believe it. . . . That's absolutely impossible!" I didn't believe it either. But it was true. And today, many years after the event, I still have no idea how to pursue the changes that occurred in your thinking.

It happened shortly after I finished college. I was still living at my father's, managing to get by one way or another by doing translations for fashion and technical magazines. Though I wanted to establish myself as a writer, I still had no confidence that I could become a novelist. And in the attempt to dodge the string of possible marriage candidates that my father paraded before me, I drew close to a young woman toward whom I felt very little emotion. I had only one condition that I required of this young woman, who later became my wife. "I'm a useless Christian myself, but if you are going to marry me, I can't have you being indifferent to my religion." I somehow held on to my faith because of my attachment to Mother. So even though I sometimes played truant from Mass and kept my distance from church, I revered the faith that my mother believed and that you lived for, and never for a moment did I consider tossing it aside. So I came to see you to ask if you would teach this young woman the doctrines of Christianity.

A trace of surprise crossed your face. I don't know if you were surprised that a fellow like me had become engaged, or if you hadn't expected someone like me to step out of character and impel another person to study Christianity. You agreed, of course, but at the time I noticed something strange. You had grown just a little bit of a scruffy beard, and your shoes were not well polished. That slackness would have seemed like nothing at all in another priest, but I couldn't imagine it happening with you. During the long war, and even during your internment at Karuizawa, you had displayed the force of your will in your raiment. Your well-brushed shoes, cleansed of every trace of dirt. You had sternly ordered each of us in the dormitory to follow your example. From my own slovenliness, I at once loathed you and held you in awe. You escorted me and the young woman to the door. There, a woman was talking to your secretary. She wore a kimono and her complexion was pallid. From a

Japanese perspective, she could not have been called a beautiful woman.

Alone I boarded a packed train and set out for the Hanshin region where I had lived with Mother. Memories of my mother were spreading their roots deeply in my mind, and I had decided to report my engagement, which I still kept secret from Father, only at Mother's grave. The neighborhood where my house once stood had been reduced to ashes by the bombing raids, my aunt's family had decided to remain in Kagawa prefecture where they were evacuated, and the majority of friends I tried calling on had disappeared. All that remained unchanged from the past were the road I had silently walked along toward the church with my mother on dark winter mornings, and the church itself. In place of the French priest, now a Japanese Father in like manner intoned Mass by himself in the deserted chapel, his shadow dancing on the walls in the light from the candles. I stood in front of the house where I lived with my mother (the house was now owned by someone from Taiwan or Korea), and I remembered your hollow face after Mother's funeral. I wondered why I had felt that a look of loss had appeared in your face, too. Then I had a glance at the pine grove where I had roamed in search of the dog you made me give up. The moist, sad expression in that dog's eyes suddenly flickered through my mind. A yellow whirlwind twisted through the burnt ruins, while an exhausted-looking man dug in the ground with a spade.

It was around this time that I first heard the preposterous rumor about you. It was an absurd slander circulated by someone who knew nothing at all about you. The gossip intimated that, although you were a member of the clergy, you had a relationship with a Japanese woman that had gone beyond the bounds of decency. When I heard the rumor, I thought of the pale Japanese woman I had seen at your doorway. But I loathed the attitude of Japanese Christians, who were quick to judge people by appearances, to measure others on mere formalities, and perpetually to regard themselves as righteous. I laughed off the gossip: "What nonsense!" Because I knew what kind of person, how strong-willed a man you were. I knew at the very least that the man my mother had respected would never do anything like that, even in the worst possible circumstances.

The rumors reached my ears from various sources. Hearsay blended with base curiosity led someone to claim they had seen you riding in your Jeep with that woman; another reported that you had been out shopping somewhere with her. I tore into the man who relayed those rumors to me. "What's wrong with their being in the same Jeep? If you've got errands to run, it's all right to be in a Jeep with a woman." He stared into my face with surprise and then blushed. "She's a divorced woman, you know." From somewhere he had information about the woman. "And she has a child." My mother was a divorced woman, too. A divorced woman with a child. That priest is the one who instilled faith in her, who taught her about a world of greater holiness—the words rose up as far as my throat, but I sealed my lips. For something distasteful, something exceedingly distasteful, had simultaneously welled up in my throat. At that time had my mother been made the object of the same kinds of slanders and rumors by the members of the Church? Had there been gossip that something had happened between her and you? I glared back into the man's face and shouted: "I don't care what anyone says. I believe in him! I believe in him!"

I believe. It's true that I believed in you. Because you had told me: "Believe in me." Even today I have not forgotten what you said to me then, or how your voice had sounded. Do you remember? When, unable to bear the petty rumors any longer, I came to your office to tell you about them. You seemed busy as always. And though you no longer had a scruffy beard, I still sensed some neglect in your dress. I couldn't put my finger on how you were neglectful. Your trousers were pressed, and the evening sunlight streaming through the window splashed against them like a blemish. Yet there was something unkempt about you that I had never detected in the past. I stood directly in front of you and reported that groundless rumors involving you were flying about. You looked up at me with a searching stare. I couldn't tell whether you were listening to what I said or not. When I finished, you were silent for a few moments. I gazed at the stain of sunlight on your trousers. Finally, with vigor, you said: "Believe in me."

You spoke the words fervently. Just as when you had said to me in the past, "Believe in Christ. Believe in God and in His Church," your voice carried the weight of heavy stones and was filled with conviction and confidence. That's how it sounded to me, at any rate. Believe. That Easter Sunday when I was baptized, I had cried out in a loud voice like the other children: "I believe!" What reason could I have had not to believe? How could I have doubted the man my mother trusted throughout her lifetime? The calm in my heart after I had received the sacrament of penance. A feeling of relief similar to that filled my heart for the first time in many months, and I could not stop myself from smiling wryly. "Goodbye." You nodded when I got up from my chair.

There were many complications in my plans to marry

the young woman, but I was finally able to persuade my father. However, he had one condition: I was not to get married in one of those "Amen" churches. How desperately my father wished to sever the psychological tie between me and Mother. I accepted his senseless request, and after I had consulted my fiancée, we decided to have two wedding ceremonies. One would be a ceremony held at a hotel for my father and his friends, the other a service at church with just the two of us. She had by then decided to be baptized. Naturally you were the one who was designated to recite the Mass for our ceremony.

The day before our secular ceremony at the hotel, I put on a plain suit that would not arouse my father's suspicion, and she dressed in a suit of the same color, and we unobtrusively called on your seminary. Just the two of us, with no one else to witness; yet I felt that from the far distance my dead mother was giving her blessing to this wedding. I wanted to boast to Mother: "If nothing else, I've turned my bride into a believer!" When we reached the front of the seminary, my fiancée took out a pure white handkerchief she had purchased without telling me, and placed it in my breast pocket. On her suit she pinned a cattleya. It was touching. "Please tell Father we're here," I instructed her.

I waited outside the chapel. It was a clear day. The Quonset hut buildings were lined up in array. Their duralumin walls glittered in the sunlight. I thought of my mother, and smiled to myself as I wondered what she might have said had she been able to meet my wife. The young woman who was about to become my wife came walking slowly toward me. Her body reeled slightly. She's really excited about this, I said grinning to myself, and threw away the cigarette that was in my mouth.

"What's up? Did you tell him we're here?"

Her face tight, she said nothing.

"Are you feeling ill?"

"No."

"Then don't look so ridiculous."

Still her face was contorted, and she would not speak. Scraping the ground with the toe of her shoe, she suddenly said: "I want to leave."

"Why?"

"Why . . . ?"

"This is no time to start talking nonsense."

Her face suddenly collapsed, and she whispered: "I saw them. I saw them," she said.

When she pushed open the door to your office to announce our arrival, you were just separating your body from that of the pale woman we had once met at your doorway. Her face had been directly beneath yours, and my fiancée left without a word, leaving the door open.

"What!" Fury pierced my chest. "That's impossible!" I slapped her across the face with an open palm. "Are you going to take part in those ridiculous rumors, too?"

She pressed her hand against her cheek. Your words came slowly back to me: "Believe in me."

The ceremony. Her eyes were red and swollen from crying. Did you think they were tears of joy? You couldn't have. You couldn't have done anything like that. As I stared at you and at the altar while you performed the Mass, I struggled to subdue the doubts that kept welling up in my chest like foul bubbles that rise to the surface of a murky swamp. "Believe in Christ," you had told me. There was no way you could recite the Mass of Christ if you had just done something like that. Even then I was trying to believe in you.

After we were married, I frequently reproached my wife when her face twisted at the memory of that morning. "Do you doubt the man my mother trusted more than anyone else?" And my wife would shake her head. But if, in fact, what she told me was true, it meant that the one pure ceremony of marriage she would ever experience had been performed by a priest with filthy hands. That would have been just too cruel. In order to distance myself from such doubts, I began avoiding you. And three months later, I heard the definitive news that you had left the seminary.

* * *

How had this happened? I was in a daze. In any case, I had to meet you and get you to tell me everything. The urge to believe in you no matter what others said mingled with a sense of betrayal to strangle my heart. But they told me at the seminary that they did not know your whereabouts. I lost my temper with them, telling them their answer was irresponsible, but there was nothing to be done. Finally, after all manner of inquiries, I learned that you were staying with one of your fellow-countrymen, a Spaniard in the import-export business.

I sent you a letter. But instead of a reply, all I received was a message from a Spaniard claiming to be your friend, asking me to leave you alone for the time being. I felt I could understand why you didn't want to see even me—no, me especially. I could imagine how isolated you felt amidst your shame and humiliation. I eventually gave up the notion of pursuing you.

But the shock I received had in no way subsided. Just what was going on? When exactly had this absurd business started? I knew none of the answers to these questions. Only one image surfaced from the depths of my memory—the scruffy, chestnut-colored beard that smudged your chin like grime the first time I brought my wife to your office. Had you, by any chance, already begun to decay then? Perhaps something invisible to the eye had already started to gnaw away imperceptibly at your way of life, at your faith. That's what I felt. Of course this amounts to nothing more than my own futile imaginings.

But why did you lie even to me, to one who made every effort to believe in you? In response to my words of caution, you had said in such a confident voice: "Believe in me." Anger and pity took turns to stab into my heart, and at times my anger led me to imagine even more fearful things—that you may have deceived me and my mother for a very long time. In every instance I rejected such thoughts, driving them from my mind.

My wife would no longer speak of you. "I'm not going to church any more. I can't believe in any of it." I could not formulate any assured retort to her murmurings. "Are you going to find fault with all of Christianity just because of one missionary?" But I knew all too well that such an answer would not satisfy even my own mind. I was not alone: many clergymen and members, at a loss to explain this unexpected occurrence, felt dazed and lowered their voices to whispers. Ultimately they closed their eyes to the whole affair, burying it beneath the ashes of silence; in other words they adopted the attitude that a lid must be placed over objects that begin to stink.

But I was in a quandary. Unlike others, I could not be satisfied with waiting for the passage of time to cancel out the rumors, or for everything to be obliterated by forgetfulness. For me, forgetting you was the same as forgetting Mother, and rejecting you was to deny the wide river that was my life up until then. Unlike many converts, I had not chosen Christianity of my own volition. For a long while my faith had in a sense been tied to my attachment to Mother and linked to my veneration of you. Those aspects of my faith were being betrayed to their very roots. At this late stage, how could I join the others in forgetting you, in covering over the problem?

So I asked a number of priests: "Please go and see him." I wanted to believe (though I still don't know whether it's true) that you had abandoned the seminary and run into the arms of a woman out of a greater faith—an act, perhaps, of even greater love. And I wanted you to prove to me that even now—no, now more than ever—you possessed even stronger faith. But such childish daydreams were soon shattered. Most of the priests rejected my request, which initially angered me. Christ had never visited the fortunate or the fulfilled. They had always told me that He had hurried to the side of those who were alone, those who were subjected to humiliation. Yet it seemed to me that, in the present circumstances, no one would extend a hand to you. But my thinking was shallow. Because when one priest finally did get in touch with you, the answer that came back was the simple phrase, "He doesn't want to see you." The priest told me: "I think it's better for you to leave him in peace for now. Don't you understand how he feels?" I finally realized my own insensitivity and egoism.

And so my lengthy association with you came to an end. When I think back on it, I am aware that over thirty years have passed since you first appeared in my room at the Charity Hospital. Your soporific sermons. Remembering how I was forced to give up my dog. My agony as I ran with you along the mountain path. The incident in the dormitory. Mother's death. Your hands, swollen with frostbite, giving me your own ration of butter in Karuizawa. Each of those moments was deposited as an essential component in the river of my life. The marks that one person leaves on the life of another. We never realize what sort of marks we leave upon the lives of others, never know what diversions we bring as they pursue their course. Just as the wind twists the shape of a pine tree planted on a sandy beach, changing the angle of its branches, you and Mother, more than anyone else, bent my life in the direction it has taken. And now you have disappeared.

I later heard through the grapevine that you were supporting yourself by becoming an instructor at an English conversation school and teaching private Spanish lessons. Someone told me that a child had been born to you and the Japanese woman. These pieces of news were absorbed into my heart with less of a sense of shock than before, and the incident that had temporarily caused such consternation among the members of the church was gradually passing from memory.

My wife and I have never again mentioned what happened before our wedding ceremony. It's not that the topic never comes up, but that we both avoid touching upon it. And yet, sometimes after we have finished dinner and I move from the kitchen to my study, closing the door tightly behind me and facing my desk; or late at night when I raise my head from a book, I suddenly hear your voice. "Believe in me." At such times I struggle to get a hold on you in some way or other in order to sustain my belief in you. That was one of the reasons I made you a character (significantly altered, of course) in three of my novels and tried in various ways to probe your mind. Perhaps, just as you led my mother to a higher plane of existence, you were tripped up in your attempt to elevate the life of that woman with the pallid complexion. At first you didn't realize that your emotions as a man were gradually mingling with your compassion and your feelings as a priest. You had too much confidence in yourself. You didn't know that a mighty tree can snap without warning. Perhaps your excess of self-assurance is what unexpectedly tripped you up. And once you stumbled, the speed with which a man like you slides down the embankment is swift. Many times I made a stab at formulating such hypothetical schemes, and each time I failed. In the final analysis, I don't understand the truth about your fall. And, yes, it's true that the wounds in my heart were not healed by setting up such suppositions.

But one day I saw you again, for the first time in many years. It was on the roof of a department store one Saturday evening. At the time I was living in Komaba, and sometimes I would take my son to the playground there on the roof. It was one of those days. My first-grade son rode around in a twirling teacup, and became engrossed in a mannequin that talked when you inserted a coin. A large circular contraption with several planes attached to it whirled to the music as the planes flew through the air. Fathers and mothers sat on a chair here, a bench there, relaxing and watching their children just as I was, and I bought myself a Coke and drank it slowly as I read my newspaper. I glanced up, and there I caught a glimpse of you from behind.

A tall wire fence had been stretched around the edge of the roof to prevent accidents. On this side of the fence were several telescopes that provided a brief view of the city when a ten-yen coin was inserted, and the children brought here by their parents had clustered round them. You were standing by yourself between the telescopes and the fence, looking out at the darkening city. A large bank of leaden clouds spread over the city, and only one slice of sky to the west glimmered a milky white, spilling a few beams of faint, forlorn sunlight. It was an utterly commonplace evening sky for Tokyo, and viewed from my angle your body appeared somewhat shorter than the buildings and apartment houses in the distance. Maybe it was due to the smog, but the lights that had been turned on in some of the windows of the buildings shone with a strange blur, and pieces of underwear and bedding were hanging out to dry outside the apartments. You no longer wore the black cassock and Roman collar of a Catholic clergyman. I think you were wearing a tattered gray suit. It may have been the suit that made me feel that your body, which had been so imposing in the past, had become somehow thin and shabby. It may be rude to use such a description, but you looked to me like some provincial foreigner. What I found unusual was the fact that I felt no particular surprise. Instead the whole thing seemed natural, something to be expected. I don't know why. The assurance and confidence you once possessed had vanished now, and none of the many ordinary Japanese parents and children who were passing the time on the roof of the department store that evening gave you even a second glance. Almost inadvertently I started to get to my feet. But just then a familiar-looking woman, tugging at the hand of a child dressed in a white knit outfit, came over to you. The two of you turned your backs on me and headed for the distant exit, walking as if you were shielding the child.

I said that I had met you, but that was all there was to it. Of course I said nothing about it to my wife. That negligible reunion has popped into my mind in recent years, often at night. And as I ponder how you looked as you stood with your back to me, that image is superimposed upon several other shadows that have crossed the river of my life. The old White Russian man selling Russian bread in Dalian when I was a child. The elderly foreigner who furtively slipped into the priest's quarters, dragging his tired legs. (That old foreigner was expelled from the priesthood for getting married, just as you were.) One summer twilight, as I tried to run away from him, he had said: "Don't be afraid of me." His plaintive eyes overlap with the eyes of the mongrel you made me get rid of. Why is it that the eyes of animals and birds are filled with such sorrow? I can't help but feel that all of these images have formed into a chain inside me, binding themselves together into blood relations, and are trying to communicate something to me. But when I make room for them in my life as a kind of chain, I can no longer think of you as a dynamic missionary brimming with confidence and conviction, nor as a man, standing between lighted buildings and apartment houses where washing hangs out to dry, who looks down on life from a higher position and passes judgment upon it. Instead, I think of you as a man whose eyes are now no different from the sad eyes of a dog. As a result, even if you did betray me, my bitterness over that has diminished. In fact, I even think that the person you once believed in came here for just such a purpose. Or perhaps you already know that. Because in that restaurant at Shibuya, with a drizzling rain falling outside, you quickly and inconspicuously crossed yourself after the waitress delivered your food. That's all I really understand about you now.

Confronting the Shadows

Propping himself with one hand on the tatami mat, Suguro flipped through the pages of the old photo album that had survived the fire at his father's house. A dank smell permeated the album, its black pages faded. There was a photograph his father had taken of Suguro as a young boy. A photo from the time they climbed Mt. Takao. A tired-looking boy with close-cropped hair stood next to his father. Another photograph taken on the shore of the Atagawa River. Here, too, he was standing with his father. Back then, his father had been the same age as Suguro was now, and in every one of the photos he wore a forced smile. (It suddenly occurred to Suguro that whenever his own photograph was taken, his faint-hearted smile was the same as his father's.) Here and there among the pictures were traces of some photos that had been torn out from where they had once been pasted. All that remained was the gray, dried residue of the glue. Suguro of course knew perfectly well who had been in those photos and who had ripped them from the album.

"Come here, Minoru. Let me hold your hand." Suguro's father held on to his grandson's hand, leading him around the tiny pond in the garden. Behind them walked Suguro's wife, conversing with his stepmother. The deep red azaleas along the edge of the pond glowed like tiny flames. The sweet flags sent up spouts from the dark ground that looked like sword blades.

"Those are koi, not goldfish. Can you count how many there are, Minoru?" Suguro's father had stopped and, holding on to Minoru from behind, was peering into the water. "There's three, four."

Suguro was unhappy that his son Minoru was clutching his grandfather's hand. He tried to squelch the feeling, knowing logically that he was being unreasonable. He lowered his eyes to the photo album and inwardly muttered to the person whose photographs had been torn out. *You died without ever seeing Minoru's face. You never had the joy of hugging Minoru. And you never saw my wife's face, either. What are you feeling right now, on this spring Sunday, as you look at my father surrounded by my wife and your grandson?*

"Two, three, four fish."

"There's another one under that rock. It's hiding!"

The sun flickered like heat haze on the surface of the water—a koi had darted past. The light shone on his father's contented face; he was wearing handmade work trousers over his kimono. Porcelain cups and the tea ceremony had always been his passions, but since his retirement he had adopted the style and even the clothing of a haiku poet.

Suguro's stepmother stroked Minoru's head and said, "It's time we had some tea. And let's have some cake in the parlor."

Picking up the photo album, Suguro started toward the storage closet, but just then his son came into the room, holding on to his grandmother's hand.

"Show me that book."

Suguro's wife called out from behind, "It's a photo album, isn't it? I've never seen that old album before."

"It's just pictures of people you don't know. Nothing worth looking at," Suguro grumbled, opening the closet door and tucking the album away on the highest shelf next to all the other items stacked in the closet.

"Why are you hiding it?"

"I told you, there's no point looking at it. It's got nothing to do with you." His wife looked resentful, but he shook his head. Inwardly he felt like saying to her, *Could you just think about this a little more?*

"What's going on?" Suguro's father, who had scurried in to have Minoru wash his hands, studied the faces of Suguro and his wife and asked suspiciously.

"It's that photo album," Suguro's wife responded without thinking. "For some reason he's hid it way up there in the closet."

His father looked down and said nothing. Without a word he took Minoru's hand and led him to the washroom. He was well aware that a number of photos had been torn from the album.

* * *

"Minoru certainly eats well, doesn't he?"

"He really does. I'm always worried that he might get an upset stomach."

"But isn't he quite a bit taller than children his age because he eats so well?"

"The doctor is very complimentary."

Suguro's wife was chattering away with self-satisfaction at the praise being heaped on her son, while his father was poking at his teeth with a toothpick.

"Did my husband eat this much when he was a child?" Suguro's wife, not sure when to stop, asked. "He doesn't have much of an appetite these days."

His wife had no idea what impact her words might have on his father and stepmother. It didn't even occur to her that it was insensitive to ask such a question in the presence of his stepmother, who knew nothing about Suguro's childhood. Suguro inwardly clicked his tongue in vexation.

"Are you serious?" With a forced look of composure, Suguro's father said, "He was always snacking. We couldn't make him stop no matter what we said to him."

Suguro's stepmother ignored the conversation and used her spoon to feed some pudding to Minoru.

"But he wasn't this skinny as a child, was he?"

"He was pretty average, I think," Suguro's father cast a glance toward his stepmother, "but as I remember he was overweight for a time when he was in college. There were food shortages back then, but Shige went out shopping a lot so she could give him something to eat."

Suguro had shown his wife some photos of himself when he was in college. But that photo album containing pictures of him as a child had been buried at the back of a closet, where it gathered dust. Once again Suguro thought of the traces left by the photographs that someone had ripped out of the album, leaving only dried, unsightly gray clumps of glue. Watching his stepmother's hands as she scooped out pudding and fed it to Minoru, he thought, *I remember the taste of the pancakes you used to make for me. When I came home from elementary school, you'd feed me pancakes dripping with that Dorikono syrup. The flavor of Dorikono.* That syrup with its caramel taste had only been around when Suguro was a child.

As he carefully picked up the bits of candy that Minoru had dropped while sitting on his lap, Suguro's father said, "Yūzō, I want to talk to you about something. Can you come with me?"

They left the parlor and went into his father's study. Everything in the room was neat and orderly, as it always had been. The bookshelves were lined with volumes containing Buddhist parables and the collected writings of the leaders of Seichō-no-Ie;[1] a brush holder, his name seal, and a large bronze paperweight were arranged on his desk. Absolutely nothing had changed over the twenty years since Suguro had been in college. All of it seemed to signify the unvarying life his father had led up to the present day. The only new item in the study was a framed calligraphy print that read "In all things, Man must be free of attachments." Suguro smiled faintly, thinking how totally inapplicable this was to his father's life.

"That? Oh, it was a present a while back."

"Whose calligraphy is it?"

"Mr. Tamura, a representative in the Lower House, wrote it for me."

Suguro had no interest in who had written it for his father. It was just that he was slightly amused that the phrase "In all things, Man must be free of attachments" had absolutely no connection with his father's life.

"What is it you wanted to talk about?"

"Well . . ." His father used a cloth to dust off a chair and said, "You know that I retired from my teaching job this year."

1. Seichō-no-Ie (literally, "House of Growth") is a Japanese new religion, founded in 1930.

"Money problems?"

"No, nothing to worry about there. I've been saving up for a long time."

Yes, of course. My father is the kind of person who would have been scrupulously preparing for his retirement for ten or fifteen years. Once there had been a calligraphy scroll by someone hanging in this room of his that read, "We have no worries if we are prepared." Suguro had known for some time that the old man had bought stocks, signed up for retiree health insurance, and purchased life insurance to take care of his wife.

"Really, a desk has to be dusted every single day, or it won't shine like this," his father stopped moving his hand for a moment and muttered. "But don't you think people are the same way? If you don't polish your abilities while you're young, once you get old there's nothing you can do about it. When I was your age, I could get away with little mistakes because of my youth, but the story's very different when you get old. That's because old people no longer have anything to offer society. And society treats us brutally. That's the bottom line."

How many times since his youth had Suguro had to listen to these maxims for success in life? His father must have delivered these homilies, seemingly appropriated from some of the books on his shelf—like the collections of Buddhist parables or writings from Seichō-no-Ie—to his students exactly as he had to Suguro.

"In fact, I've tried my hand at writing something myself recently. Even an old man can't idle away his time." He took a large paper sack from under his desk and showed it to Suguro.

"What have you written?"

"It's a sort of biography of Li Shangyin."[2]

Suguro opened the hefty paper sack that his father handed him. It weighed about what a hundred or so handwritten manuscript sheets would weigh. The tiny characters were a perfect reflection of his father's timid nature. There were no signs of mistakes or corrections. With one single exception, there had been no mistakes or corrections in his father's life. What could possibly be the point for such a man to write anything?

"This must have been hard to write," Suguro said with a wan smile.

"At some point I'd like to publish it."

"Do you have a publisher in mind?"

"That's what I wanted to ask you to help me with." His father abruptly flashed a fawning smile. "Given the choice, well, I've been thinking that a publisher like Akebono would be good."

Akebono Press was a first-rate publisher. There was no way Suguro could take them something written by an unknown old man and expect them to jump at the chance to publish it.

"But a hundred sheets isn't enough to turn into a book. Generally speaking, when we're talking book-length works . . ." Suguro tried to squeeze out of the situation, but his father ignored him and added, "Of course, this is only a third of the whole thing."

Out of sorts, Suguro lit a cigarette. He was a translator of detective novels, and he hoped someday to be able to have a

2. Li Shangyin was a Chinese poet and politician (circa 813–858) active during the rapid decline of the Tang dynasty.

company like Akebono publish one of his works. And here his father was asking him to do something Suguro himself hadn't been able to do. He did not have the influence to bring his father's manuscript to Akebono. Even worse, he remembered something that had happened twenty years earlier. His father, who was opposed to his son's wish to study literature, had encouraged him to choose a stable path in life. In the end, he was booted out of his father's house for a period of two years and had to live elsewhere.

Around eight o'clock, after multiple efforts to calm down Minoru, who had started to fuss, he left his father's house. Suguro led his son out by the hand, his wife following behind and carrying their Boston bag.

"It wasn't until afterward that I realized it," she suddenly admitted as they walked along the unlit street. "I understood why you didn't let me look at that photo album. I'm sorry. It was thoughtless of me."

When he did not reply, she tried to make it clear that she sympathized with him. "You really had to walk on eggshells when you lived in that house, didn't you?"

"You know nothing about it." He spit on the roadway. He was upset that his wife had had a glimpse of how he was regarded in that house. "Just forget about it and take Minoru's other hand."

"I wonder why Mother—of course I'm talking about your late Mother—left your father."

Suguro did not respond. That secret was his and his alone. He didn't want even his wife prying into his memories of his mother.

* * *

Why had his mother left his father? At this stage of his life he could imagine her reasons. But it was still only guesswork. Since it was impossible to plumb the depths of someone else's heart, his conjectures could do little more than skim the surface of the truth of his mother's secrets. But inwardly, the more he idealized his memories of her, the more he felt contempt toward his father and was determined to probe to the degree possible the reasons why his mother had left her husband.

About four years earlier, while in Kobe on business, he had made up his mind to visit the place where his mother had grown up. (*I was told that my mother had once taken me there when I was young, but I don't remember much of anything about it.*) Suguro was one of the few people to disembark at the train station, which was so tiny that the train stopped for only two minutes and then set out again. The autumn sun shone abundantly on the platform where a riot of white cosmos flowers bloomed against the black fence. A single truck was parked in the plaza in front of the station. Although he had gotten off the train, he had no idea which direction to head.

He suddenly remembered that his mother's cousin, Tatsu-san, still lived here, and when he asked the truck driver if he knew where Tatsu-san's house might be, the driver was quick to direct him. He walked across the plaza swarming with red dragonflies.

His mother's cousin, a country doctor about fifty-five or fifty-six years in age, greeted him with a look of surprise. In the garden a large crape myrtle tree was lit by the afternoon sun, and cicadas were still buzzing on its trunk.

"Your mother?" He nodded, an Asahi cigarette clutched

between his teeth. "I don't remember anything about her other than when she was going to that girls school."

"I'd like to hear anything you remember."

"Do you know about her leaving home?"

Suguro had heard only a little about it. She had been studying the violin since she was a student at the girls school. After graduation she hoped to be accepted by the music school at Ueno in Tokyo. When her parents violently opposed her plan, one day she suddenly fled from the house. She started working as a maid for a family in Himeji to make the money for her travel and living expenses so she could study violin at the music school in Tokyo.

"It wouldn't be like this today, but that became a major topic of gossip in this country town." As he poured some sencha, Tatsu-san continued, "After all, for a daughter of a wealthy family in the village to be working as a maid, it tells you that your mom was already a bit out of the ordinary. Stubborn, you might say, determined to do things her way."

"Stubborn."

"Well, she was definitely strong-willed."

Suguro did not respond, sensing from Tatsu-san's tone of voice that the man was not recalling his mother with fondness, but rather with strong disdain.

Perhaps it wasn't disdain, but it felt as though Tatsu-san didn't know how to deal with the way Suguro's mother had lived her life. And Tatsu-san wouldn't have been the only one who had that problem. His mother's parents and siblings would doubtless have felt the same way toward her back then. He closed his eyes and summoned up her shadowy silhouette from his memory.

He went to see the elementary school she had attended so many years before. Back then, it had likely been constructed of dark wood, but now a squarish white concrete building stood in its place. Children were playing jump rope in the schoolyard. From midway up the mountainside where the school stood, one could look down over the entire village. Tatsu-san said that the village looked nothing like it once had due to the damaging fires from the war, but Suguro thought he could understand why his mother did not want to live out her entire life in this tiny, closed-off village buried deep in the mountains.

* * *

Suguro placed the manuscript of one of his translations in a bundle, and as he was walking past his wife, he noticed that she had stripped Minoru naked and was applying talcum powder to his arms and sides.

"He's got heat rash and here it's only May. I wonder if I should get some peach tree leaves from our landlady."

He didn't reply as he opened the dusty shoe box in the entryway and took out a pair of shoes with worn soles. The tacks sticking through the soles stabbed at the bottoms of his feet.

"You're going out?"

"I'm going to my publisher," he answered grumpily. "Listen, you need to dust this shoe box. Look at how the mud and dust has collected inside. And take these shoes to the repair shop tomorrow. The heels are totally worn down."

"Okay, okay. . . . But you know that your shoes wear out on the right side very quickly. The problem is the way you walk." Hoping to humor him, she said, "They say that people whose shoes wear out that way are cowardly and weak of heart . . ."

The tacks bit into the soles of his feet several times as he walked to the road where the bus stopped. With each jab, Suguro grimaced and stopped walking. For some reason, he was reminded of what his wife had just said about cowardice. Although she had thoughtlessly said it as a jest, it had hit him hard. It stung mostly because six years earlier, he had taken this young woman to a coffee shop in Shibuya, where he had tried to present himself as a young man who faced life with courage. He spouted off the names of authors she had never heard of and grumbled at how dull their novels were, and he had gone so far as to claim that one day he would write a work better than any of theirs. Had she been beguiled by his claims? Only a month later, she agreed to marry him.

But five years into their marriage . . . not a single one of his stories had appeared in print. No matter how many newcomer prizes he applied for, he had won none. Initially he felt bitter that the awards judges didn't appreciate his talent, but as one failure followed another, the dust of weariness gradually collected on his life like that on his shoe box, and the desire to become a novelist at some point turned into resignation. Because he was at least good at languages, he somehow managed to feed his family by translating mystery novels. Suguro was more conscious than anyone else of the posture he had assumed over time.

(Cowardly and weak of heart)

Maybe that criticism was how she actually viewed him. Although the words had sprung from her subconscious mind, they felt to Suguro like she meant them, precisely because they had come from her subconscious.

When he finished his business at the publishers, he headed for a second-floor bar in Kanda. A regular gathering of his friends, all of whom were trying to write novels, was held there. When he arrived, six or seven of the men were conversing about something as they sipped saké.

"Suguro. You still haven't paid your group dues this month," Atagawa said.

"Ah!" Suguro flushed slightly. "Sorry, but can you wait a little longer? If I pay you now, I won't have anything left to buy a drink here."

Everyone laughed when Atagawa clicked his tongue, giving Suguro up as hopeless. These men were genial, but sensing that not one of them had any talent, he listened as Atagawa and Bitō disparaged the popular writers as vulgarians. Suguro knew full well that their insults came less from criticism than from jealousy.

When their gathering concluded, Suguro went with Fujii, who was headed in the same direction, to catch a train.

"Suguro," the young Fujii said as he dangled from the train car strap, "You aren't writing anything recently, are you?"

"I'm going to write," Suguro responded with annoyance. "Any day now."

"I guess it's true that you just have to write something every month. And I suppose if you're going to produce literature, you've got to be persistent, don't you?" Fujii muttered in stops and starts as he gazed out the train window. Suguro had the vague sense that once long ago, before he was even married, he had been as enthusiastic as this Fujii fellow. That eagerness had now faded from his heart without a trace, and since his marriage, a white dust had gradually accumulated atop his life. The only reason Suguro was just barely holding on to his association with his old comrades is because he felt that if this slender thread were severed, he would give up entirely on literature.

When he returned home, his wife was doing some mending while she sat beside a sleeping Minoru. "I've heated up the bath for you," she said.

When he undressed, his wife glanced up at him and chuckled, "The spitting image."

"What is?"

"Minoru and you. He's got a bit of that stooped back that you have."

He looked down at his sleeping son, whose face was slaked with perspiration. He didn't need his wife to tell him that Minoru's physique resembled his own. Suguro's father and grandfather were of the same build, so he supposed it should be called hereditary. Each time Suguro shared the bath with his son, he sensed the inescapable ties of blood that left him feeling cheerless. He wasn't yet sure how Minoru would turn out, but at times he realized that beyond just the shape of his body, even some of his trivial gestures and habits very much resembled those of his own father.

"When you see the way I walk," he asked his wife, "doesn't it remind you of my father?"

"It does. Really."

"And when you look at me, do you think there are ways in which I'm exactly like my father?"

"Hmm." His wife tilted her head, considering his question. "Just the other day, when I saw your father digging at his ear with his finger while he was reading the newspaper, I thought, ah, like father like son."

"Why?"

"You realize you often do the same thing, don't you?"

Ever since his schooldays he had hated that habit of his father, who had painstakingly grown out the nail on his little finger. He looked so petty when he pored intently over each page of the newspaper, digging at his ear with that nail, giving the impression of an old man who was utterly content with his risk-free daily life. Suguro had been determined to never adopt such a pose no matter how old he got. But once his wife pointed it out, he had to agree that, indeed, somewhere along the line he had adopted the same distasteful habit.

That night, as he listened to his wife sleeping soundly beside him, he thought about the traits that he had inherited from his father and mother. His wife's breathing was regular, and the night was quiet. He couldn't yet say what he had inherited from his mother, but he felt he knew what he had received from his father. His stooped posture, the cowardice and timidity that made him want to settle into a daily routine that would somehow enable him to just get by—those were traits he had likely inherited from his father. He despised the fact that he was prone to those tendencies, but mere disdain for his father was insufficient: he made every effort to fight back by hating his father at such times.

One day, with his chin resting on his hands and a cigarette dangling from his mouth, he asked his wife, "If you were ever to leave me, when would it be?"

She gave him a rather disgusted look as she cleaned the glass door with a rag. Even after she pulled her hand away, the glass in the door continued to rattle.

"What an odd thing to ask out of the blue. Do you feel like leaving me?"

"That isn't why I asked you. I'm just saying supposing you did."

"Well, I guess I might leave you if I stopped believing in myself."

"What do you mean by stopped believing?"

"Well, for example, if you took up with another woman, and she turned out to be so much better than me. But it would be hard since we have a child. Women are vulnerable, we can't so easily give up our current lives."

Suguro had been thinking about his father as he peered at the purple smoke climbing up through his fingertips. In the eyes of the world, his father had certainly not been a bad husband. Logically he understood that. Had he secretly cheated on Suguro's mother? No, given the man's timid personality, there wasn't any way he could have touched a woman other than his wife out of fear of losing his job as a teacher at the high school. From the worldly perspective there was no way that his mother had been betrayed by his father.

(But had he been disloyal to her in some other way?)

Suguro stole a look at his wife's back. All he needed to do to understand his father was to exaggerate some of the man's traits that resided within himself. His wife, unaware of what he was thinking, continuing cleaning energetically with her rag.

"Hey."

"What?"

"Aren't you dissatisfied with our life right now?"

She turned back to look at Suguro with surprise in her eyes. "Why would I be? We're not ever lacking for anything."

"No, that's not what I'm talking about." He looked at the floor. "Years ago, I . . ."

He started to ask whether she was unhappy with the differences between how he had been before they had married compared to after, but it was clearly too embarrassing as her husband to ask such a question. Didn't you marry me because you thought I would become a man of character? Didn't you marry me not knowing that I was a cowardly man at heart?

"Well," she said, continuing to wipe away at the glass, either knowing nothing of what was in Suguro's mind or perhaps deliberately pretending not to know, "there'd be no end to it if I listed off things I've wanted. But lately I've started thinking that really the greatest happiness comes when nothing at all is happening."

* * *

It was snowing. New snow was falling atop the already frozen layer of snow. The wind was blowing black smoke across the snow. The wrist and the five fingers continued moving like machinery. The fingers incessantly glided from the edge of one string to another. It wasn't because of the fingers pressing down on the strings; the tips of the nails were forcing that piercing sound out into space. One single melody was being played over and over for three hours. Only the chin supported the violin, while the teeth chewed on the lower lip. The child watched his mother's stern face with trepidation.

"Can I have something to eat?" he asked. "Don't we have any fruit?"

In truth, he wasn't interested in fruit. All he wanted was to draw his mother's attention toward him. He wanted her to speak to him.

"Can I have something? Please . . . ?"

But she continued to stroke her bow across the violin as though unable even to hear her child's voice. Because her mind was completely focused on her five fingers until she could locate the one sound she was pursuing, she couldn't hear anything resembling the voice of a child.

"I'm asking you whether we have any fruit?"

The child shook his mother. He was so upset that he had forgotten how strictly she had forbidden him to speak to her or make any noise while she was playing her violin.

"What are you doing?!" She glared at Suguro with a terrifying face. She pointed toward the hallway with her bow and ordered him to stand out there and not move. The area below her chin had turned a bright red. Blood had pooled beneath her skin thanks to the violin that had been tucked there for three hours.

"If you can't listen to my orders, you can go stand out in the snow."

The child backed away dejectedly, tears pooling in his eyes. This was one memory of his mother from Suguro's childhood.

When he related this experience to his wife, she gave a deep sigh. "I could never do anything like that. Weren't you frightened?"

"I was scared of my mother when she was that way," Suguro nodded. "Her right arm was thicker than her left arm, and I can still remember very clearly that the skin on the tips of her five fingers was stiff and gray from being mashed against the strings of her violin."

"No, no, that's not what I'm talking about. I'm saying that I could never scold a child of mine when he was hungry. Never."

Realizing that his wife was being critical of his mother, Suguro's face stiffened. *I'm the only one who is allowed to crit-*

icize her. He lowered his eyes and inwardly grumbled, *What makes you think you can presume to understand my mother? Those times when I was trying to write a novel, you'd clomp around the house. And no matter how many times I'd ask you not to, you'd come barging in to pass along some pathetic rumor from the neighborhood. Even now you have no idea how much your footsteps and your voice would throw me off track and hamper my ability to think about the novel I was writing. So what makes you think it's okay for* you *to judge her anger at such times?*

"You think too highly of your late mother." Then his wife quickly added, "Of course, that's pretty normal for a man."

Begrudgingly, Suguro had to acknowledge his wife's criticism of his mother. How many times in the past had he tried to write a novel about his father and mother? But ultimately, as he began scribbling along the manuscript paper, he realized that no matter how hard he tried, he couldn't shake off unkind feelings toward his father or an overly indulgent view of his mother, and he gave up the attempt to write any further. In the case of his mother, he romanticized even things that appeared to others as intolerable faults. When it came to her, there was no way he could do what critics often described as "writing without idealizing your characters."

But the image of his mother from thirty years earlier, searching for that one sound for three, even four hours as her child Suguro looked on, or her hands as they mechanically moved without ceasing over the strings, and the crushed fingertips that were like leather—as such memories arose time and time again, they became something more than mere nostalgia for Suguro. His mother, her brows rumpled in dissatisfaction as she determinedly chased after that single melody. His mother, trying to produce something beyond music with her fingertips.

* * *

"I came to Shibuya to do some shopping, so I thought I'd stop by for a bit."

Suguro's father came in through the garden carrying a shopping bag. He sat down on the veranda, took off the Panama hat he had worn for many years, and painstakingly wiped it with the sleeve of his suit jacket. A red crease from the hat was still visible on his sweaty forehead.

"What's Minoru up to?"

"He's just recently learned how to draw with crayons. He's over in his room right now totally absorbed in his drawing."

"Have him come out here."

Placing Minoru on his lap, his father used one hand to untie the string on a paper-wrapped package. "These have fresh cream in them, but they were made today, so they're okay to eat. Oh, and so I hear that you've started drawing pictures, have you? Sometime I'd like you to try to draw grandpa's face."

Hoping perhaps to humor her father-in-law, Suguro's wife went and got two or three sheets of art paper that Minoru had scribbled on with crayons. "Here's some things he's drawn."

"Oh!" He took an eyeglass case from the inside pocket of his jacket and put on a pair of senior glasses. His movements were so typical of an elderly man. "These are very good for a five-year-old."

"Are they?" His wife's delighted smile irritated Suguro.

"This boy might have artistic talent. If he does, it's your duty to develop his talent to the fullest."

Trying to avoid notice, Suguro clenched his fists as they rested on his lap. A memory from over a dozen years or so earlier had suddenly burst into his chest. He had been sitting across from his father in his study with the *Buddhist Parables* collection on the bookshelves.

"Listen to me, don't even think about writing a novel. Something like that is okay as a hobby, but you can't make a career of it."

As was his wont, his father started his lecture with a patient attempt to persuade his listener. As long as his listener did not respond, his father would press on, intoxicated by his own voice. Suguro sat with his hands on his knees, listening quietly, his eyes lowered.

"There are many risks inherent in a profession like that. For starters, say you end up unable to feed yourself, then what would you do? As a rule, normal people keep their distance from the arts."

He wasn't sure whether his father was thinking of his mother when he used the phrase "normal people." But it felt to Suguro as though his father's words were meant as an indictment of his mother.

"You're thinking about pursuing such a career because you don't yet understand anything about the world. Fellows who get involved in the world of novels or paintings eventually end up dying miserable deaths. An uneventful life is best. An uneventful life is the happiest life."

It was true that his mother had died a miserable death. Seen through his father's eyes or the eyes of the society that validated his father's life, her later years had indeed been filled with misery. No doubt his father was hinting at her sufferings.

"Don't you think it'd be best if you became a teacher like I did?"

"I think I have the right to choose my own line of work."

"Don't be ridiculous. I won't allow such selfishness so long as I'm feeding you and paying your tuition. If you really want to become a novelist, tomorrow won't be too soon for you to have a shot at making your own money and feeding yourself."

Suguro did not forget a single word of that admonition over the next decade or more. Even today he resented the simple rebuke from his father that an ordinary child would eventually bury deep in his memory; it had been more than a mere reproach of his son, but felt to Suguro as though it implied contempt for his mother. "Fellows who get involved in the world of novels or paintings eventually end up dying miserable deaths."

It was true that his mother had died unattended by anyone in the dreary apartment where she had been living. When Suguro got the news and rushed to her apartment, only the bewildered old woman who managed the apartment and had phoned him sat helplessly beside his mother's body. Dark shadows of pain were etched between the brows of his dead mother's face, which was drained of blood and more pallid than a sheet of paper.

"If this boy says he wants to become an artist, I'll help him out."

Suguro continued to gaze at the *aralia* shrubs growing in his garden, but he twisted his lips at the irony.

"Yes, that's a good idea. I've heard that these days, an artist can make a lot of money in fields like industrial design. Evidently they make a lot more money than people like you in the translation business."

What a damn smooth talker you are, Suguro grumbled to himself, but his wife said, "My husband has a friend who's in that line of work, and he's even bought himself a vacation home."

"Really, a vacation home!"

Tiny scraps of paper and bits of thread were scattered around the roots of the *aralia* in his garden. No matter how often he'd told his wife not to sweep dust from the room into the garden when she cleaned, as recently as today she must have taken the lazy route. There had been a potted rubber tree in the room where his mother died. The leaves of the tree were a withered yellow in color, and scraps of trash and string had fallen around its roots.

* * *

One day while he was still in school, Suguro stumbled across a pocket-sized edition of the Man'yōshū collection of ancient poetry in the closet that the family photo album had been tossed into.[3] It was one volume from a collection of classical Japanese literature, which can sometimes turn up even today in the corner of a used bookstore in Kanda. The scents of moisture and mold drifted up as he flipped through the pages. On the back of the inside cover Suguro discovered the names of his father and his mother written in almost totally faded ink. A few seconds passed before he realized that the names were written in his father's youthful hand. A thin, amused smile spread across his cheeks when he read a love poem from the Man'yōshū that had been inscribed to the left of the two names. Because it was a poem he had learned in

3. The Man'yōshū collection, compiled circa 759, contained more than four thousand poems.

high school, he initially wondered why his father had bothered to write it, but then another faint smile appeared on his face. The smile lingered there as Suguro stared at the characters written in two lines. He wasn't smiling because of the humorous fact that his father had written such a love poem to his mother. When his father was in a good mood, he would often say things like, "A young man has foolish thoughts because he knows nothing of the world," and he would nod in self-satisfaction. But his father had done the same sort of foolish things in his youth.

Suguro was smiling because in those faded ink characters he could sense the feelings of inferiority of a college student who had come to Tokyo from the northeast. He had gone to the trouble of buying a copy of the Man'yōshū as a present for his fiancée. And on the inside cover he had written a love poem known to every middle school student. That pretentious, unpolished approach captured for Suguro an image of his father in his youth.

But, what about his mother . . . ?

Why did his mother even get engaged to his father? Did she never once realize that the man who would become her husband was a man innately far removed from the sentiments expressed in this love poem?

In subsequent years, each time he thought about what he had discovered in the poetry collection, he felt something akin to anxiety. Was he in fact doing just what his wife had called "romanticizing" his memories of his mother in her younger days? In her youth, had his mother perhaps been like any ordinary girl, swooning over hackneyed books and poems written inside their covers? The thought made him feel a kind of shadow obscuring the image he had conjured up of his mother in her later years, and he shook his head to dispel the feeling.

Minoru and Suguro's father were eating some candy the boy's grandfather had bought for him. The crease from the brim of his hat, like growth rings on a tree, was still visible on his forehead. Just as those rings accumulate on a tree, at one point in time his father had gifted a copy of the Man'yōshū to his mother, but those days had been completely buried beneath the rings of all the intervening years. Even his father probably never thought about those days. Neither was there any way for him to compare the time of his life when he had done such things with the man he was today, or even to determine which was his true self. Holding his grandson on his lap, his father was now a happy man, while his mother, having never even seen her grandson, had died in her room in an apartment building. That made Suguro unbearably angry. Then recognizing in himself the fact that he even hated that his father was happy made him gasp in surprise.

* * *

More snow was falling atop the already frozen layer of snow. The wind was blowing the black smoke from chimneys across the snow. Come November in Dalian, every house lit fires in a stove or a *pechka* oven. The soot and smoke from the *pechkas* stained the snow gray. Suguro pressed his face to the window and watched as the wind whipped by. Smoke was rising from the brick chimney in the house across the way. The sky lowered, as though stuffed with worn-out cotton batting. Again today when he returned home from school the sound of violin music echoed from the parlor. As always—tirelessly repeating, repeating, repeating the same single melody. Sometimes it suddenly screeched to a stop. That happened when his mother was unhappy with the way she was playing. The young Suguro could almost see before his eyes the angry, frustrated expression on her face.

Because he was strictly prohibited from going into the parlor while she was practicing, he couldn't see his mother when he got home from school. This harsh treatment might make other children feel lonely, but Suguro was completely used to it since it was the way things were every day. He got a mandarin orange from their Manchu maid (his mother had forbidden her to give him candy), and as he peeled it, he tried to sneak a glance of the parlor through the window, but he couldn't see his mother and was only able to hear the sound of her violin.

The neighbor's dog was racing erratically through the snow. The fur on its back was already dusted a pure white. Suguro whistled, but the dog didn't bother to look in his direction. Numerous times he had begged his mother to get him a dog, but she hadn't yet granted his request.

He heard footsteps in the garden. It was his father, the shoulders of his overcoat and his fedora daubed white with snow. When he reached the outside of the window of the parlor where he could hear the sound of the violin, he stopped and stared for a few moments in the direction from which the music was coming, but then he headed with bent back toward the rear door.

"Should I tell your wife that you're home?"

"No, it's fine. She practicing . . ."

Suguro could hear the conversation in the kitchen between his father and the Manchu maid. His father stepped out into the hallway, put his hands into his pockets, and quietly called, “Hello!” to Suguro, whose face was still pressed against the window. Then with clumsy fingers his father removed his Western-style suit and hung it in the wardrobe.

“What have you been doing?”

“Nothing.” Suguro shook his head.

“As soon as you get home from school, you’ve got to start right in on your homework.”

“We don’t have any homework today.”

“Have you seen your mother?”

“Not yet. You know I can’t go in the parlor when she’s practicing.”

Without replying, his father peered down at his son’s face. Then in a soft voice he asked, “Don’t you ever get lonely?”

“Why would you ask that?”

Suguro couldn’t understand why his father would suddenly ask such a question. His days seemed normal to him. His father, with both hands in his obi, stood next to Suguro and watched absent-mindedly as flakes continued to fall atop the frozen snow.

That same year, his mother held a recital in the Young People’s Hall. Her friends, and even people they did not know, attended in great numbers, including one white-haired foreigner. He was the Russian Mogilevsky, who was his mother’s teacher. Suguro was brought in by their family’s maid and placed in a seat at the edge of the hall so that he wouldn’t disturb others. He was dressed in a Western-style suit with sleeves too short for his arms. Now he had only jumbled memories of his mother playing several pieces on the program.

Midway through the program, he needed to use the bathroom and slid quietly out of his seat. He went out into what he thought was a deserted corridor, but his father was seated in a vacant chair facing the wall. A lonely shadow hovered over his father's back, as though no one would have anything to do with him. Staring at the lighted end of a cigarette that he wasn't smoking, his father could hear the sound of applause coming from the concert hall, but he showed no signs of moving from his spot.

* * *

His memories of the following year were linked to the first serious illness he had ever experienced. Just before summer break, his body felt listless even when he was at school. After the afternoon physical exercise class, he felt as though something was stuck in his throat. He went to the school nurse's office, where they took his temperature, which was over 101. A doctor came to see him, looked into his throat, and asked him several questions. Then a female teacher took him to the Mantetsu General Hospital, the largest facility in Dalian.

His fever persisted for several days, and each time he opened his watery, bloodshot eyes, he thought he could see swarms of insects crawling along the walls of his hospital room, and among those insects hovered his mother's pale face, her eyes peering at him. Her fingers, hardened on the strings of her violin, adjusted an icebag on his forehead and spooned soup into his mouth. She was still at his side when he opened his eyes in the middle of the night. That had almost never happened before in Suguro's lifetime.

"Summer vacation is coming right up, so it's great that you didn't miss many days of school," his mother said. "You'll be able to go back to school as soon as the new term starts."

Was he going to have to stay in the hospital that long? He asked his mother, and with a look of concern his mother nodded her head. Truth be told, Suguro didn't want to get better quickly; he was hoping instead that his hospital stay would be extended. He knew in his child's mind that it was thanks to his illness that he was able to monopolize his mother's time. It was essential that he not get well so that he could steal his mother away from her violin. The windowsill was lined with several flowerpots, including one that contained his mother's prized rubber tree. But one day when his fever had subsided, he suddenly opened his eyes from a nap and looked toward his mother. She was sitting in a chair, oblivious to him, with her elbows propped on her knees while she restlessly vibrated the fingers of her left hand. When he realized what she was doing, loneliness and anger welled up together in his heart. He shouted at his mother to change his sweat-soaked hospital gown and continued to grouse even after she changed it: he didn't like this gown, either. Finally his mother left the room in a huff.

It was while he was hospitalized that his father's older sister and her husband moved from Mukden to Dalian. What lingered in Suguro's memory for the more than twenty years since that time were the squabbles at the hospital between his aunt and his mother. Young Suguro couldn't understand why they had suddenly started to quarrel when at first they had talked in such familiar terms, but he did recall that his aunt had twisted up her mouth, which was packed with gold teeth, and said, "It's fine for you to want to play the violin, but I think a woman's primary job is to keep her house in order."

He didn't remember how his mother had responded to

this acerbic comment. What he remembered was the quivering in his mother's hands as she clenched a handkerchief above her knees.

"And don't you think this boy got sick," his aunt continued to press for an answer, "because you were so caught up in your music that you weren't looking after him?"

Suguro wasn't sure whether his father had put those words in his sister's mouth or whether it was something she had felt for some time. He didn't know if these words awakened in his mother a sense of how she was seen by others. In any case, Suguro woke up in the middle of that night feeling her fingers on his forehead. She was crying. He stiffened in bed and pretended not to notice.

When he came home from the hospital, his mother had stopped playing the violin. Like any good mother, she often made him pancakes when he got home from school. She would drench them in *dorikono* syrup.

* * *

The mystery novel he had finished translating three months earlier had started to sell considerably more copies than he thought it would. Its sales would hardly place it on a best seller list, but sales picked up after one or two weekly magazines published reviews of the book. Since he had been paid a flat fee for the translation, his payment would be the same no matter how many printings the book went through, but the publisher generously sent him an additional twenty thousand yen.

He headed into the city with his wife and son. It was a festival day, and the streets were overflowing with crowds of people. Policemen stood at crosswalks throughout the city, controlling the processions of demonstrators who sang as they marched down the streets.

They let their son play on the rooftop rides of a department store. The three of them rode in a gigantic spinning teacup. They hopped on an airplane that slowly climbed into the sky. From the airplane they could see the gray streets of Tokyo stretching far into the distance.

The twenty thousand yen he had received for the translation quickly disappeared after he bought an obi for his wife and a foreign-made fountain pen for himself. *What a shame! I didn't need an obi,* his wife kept muttering, with a look half pleased and half regretful, but Suguro responded, *Don't be miserly. You've been wanting one for some time now.*

At the store's restaurant he bought pancakes for his son and an ice cream cone for his wife. Gazing down through the window as he drank a beer, he saw that the parade of demonstrators had ended, replaced by throngs of families ambling along the streets. A feeling like contentment slowly swelled within him.

As she licked her ice cream, Suguro's wife said, "This is the first time we've indulged ourselves like this as a family."

"It's a good thing to do occasionally. We ought to do it every once in a while."

As he answered, Suguro suddenly wondered why there should be anything wrong with this kind of life. *Why do I need to write a novel at this point in my life? I'm getting along just fine right now, aren't I? Why should I feel ashamed that I'm spending these days this way?* Just then, like some cruel joke, the image of his mother's face in death popped into his head.

* * *

For a long time, his mother did not play her violin. The dark reddish-brown instrument, along with its mute and bow, lay in its case in a corner of the parlor. Sometimes, when his mother wasn't home, Suguro would nervously sneak in and quietly open the case to look at the violin. With its strings removed, the violin looked forlorn; threads that resembled the white hair of an old woman dangled from the tip of the bow.

Unlike earlier days, his mother gave directions to the Manchu maid while she fixed meals, planted flowers in the garden, and helped Suguro with his homework. Recalling those days, Suguro had less of a sense of his mother's loneliness, feeling instead that life with her now that she was once again a part of the family had been intensely happy.

His father seemed to feel similarly contented. On Sundays, he knelt by the flower bed, spending hours pulling up weeds and planning tulip bulbs. A Manchu peddler passed in front of the house, trying in broken Japanese to sell some of the prawns that filled his basket to overflowing. Pure white flowers blossomed on the acacias in their garden, and Suguro amused himself by sticking a cluster of the flowers into a perfume bottle his mother had given him. A new issue of *Shōnen Club* magazine had arrived at the local bookstore about a week after it appeared in Japan. When he got home from school, he worked until sunset drawing cartoons based on "The Adventures of Dankichi" and "Hinomaru Hatanosuke" in the magazine.

"The ordinary life is best." His father, having perhaps read those words in some book, repeated them endlessly back in those days. "No one in the family is sick, no one quarrels—that's what real happiness is. People who mock what's ordinary will one day have to eat their words. Man must never set his sights too high."

Suguro wasn't sure whether his father had searched out these words in some book so he could use them to admonish his mother. He had no memory of the look on his mother's face when he repeated them to her.

Not, of course, that there had never been small arguments between his parents. For instance, at the end of the month his father, flipping through the pages of her household account book, impatiently flicked the beads on the abacus he held in one hand. Then the disparaging lecture would commence, delivered in a soft voice. His mother listened without saying a word. When the lecture was finished, Suguro's mother, seeing the worried look on her son's face as he peered at the two of them, smiled sadly at him. Except for such minor squabbles, it appeared even to Suguro's youthful eyes that his parents were living the placid lives of any ordinary married couple.

Summers and winters were the longest seasons in Dalian's continental climate. Whenever he thought about summers in Dalian, Suguro invariably recalled the great city square and the West Park that were exposed to the strong direct sunlight. Midday, coolies naked to the waist stretched out on the ground, sleeping beneath the withered leaves of the acacia trees; streets were all but deserted; at every street corner empty carriages were parked, waiting for passengers while their horses, with all but hairless legs, stamped their feet and flicked flies away with their tails. On one such day, Suguro's mother, carrying a parasol, took him for a walk without saying a word to him. She just kept walking, saying nothing. Even when Suguro attempted to speak to her, she would merely nod sadly but give no response. Even when he asked where they were going, she just shook her head. Finally they went into a milk bar, where she bought him a dish of ice cream, but she was lost in thought and didn't even try to pick up a spoon.

"What's wrong?" Suguro stopped eating his ice cream and looked up at his mother's face. "You seem kinda low. Are you sick?"

She smiled sadly, shook her head and said, "Don't worry about me." On their way back home, she bought a swimming float, promising him that if the skies were clear on the following Sunday, she would take him swimming in the ocean.

Their lives continued in this manner for a year. No one thought it strange that his mother had quit playing the violin. There was no longer anyone who thought it unusual when they saw that, like any other housewife, she had thrown herself into the minutiae of daily life and helped Suguro with his homework. When colleagues from the Southern Manchurian Railways Company where his father was working at the time came over for an evening, Suguro's mother, assisted by the Manchu maid, brought in bottle after bottle of saké no matter how late the hour. When their guests got drunk and began singing war songs at the top of their lungs, she watched them with that familiar, forlorn smile on her face.

Was it the winter of that same year when Miss Saga, one of his mother's friends at the music school, visited Dalian? The woman had already achieved fame in Japan as a violinist, so every seat was sold out when she performed at the Young People's Hall where Suguro's mother had once held a recital. The hall was packed with young workers from the Southern Manchurian Railways Company, starved for anything redolent of Japan. After the concert, Miss Saga came to spend the night at Suguro's house. Because Suguro was put to bed in between his mother and Miss Saga, he was able to hear every word of the conversation that passed between the two women in the dark.

"I never imagined . . . ," Miss Saga, lying on her stomach, said as she lit a cigarette, "I never imagined that this is how you would end up. You don't play at all?"

"I can't play. My fingers just don't have it anymore."

"Are you happy?"

I'm completely satisfied, his mother answered distinctly. Suguro, staring at the red flame of the cigarette that waved in the darkness, was delighted to hear that answer. Thinking back on it now, he was convinced that his mother's answer was motivated by feelings of antagonism toward her former schoolmate, but there was no way that a fifth grader could have fathomed the emotions underlying his mother's reply.

* * *

A minor incident occurred during the summer of the following year. Perhaps "incident" is too strong; it would have meant nothing to anyone who had failed to notice it, but Suguro felt that it had delivered a shock to his mother. His father's youngest brother took advantage of his summer break to visit Dalian. He was still in college, but he was involved in several left-wing activities, and according to the letter they received from Suguro's grandfather, he seems to have been frequently tailed by the police.

"When Eizō gets here, I've got to give him a piece of my mind," Suguro's father said to his wife, folding up his father's letter with a sour look on his face. "He's been poisoned by some vile philosophy . . . and it sounds as though he's been neglecting his studies."

Every aspect of life was clearly divided up in the mind of Suguro's father. The differences between evil thoughts and good thoughts, between acceptable behavior and things that must never be done was crystal clear to him. For him, one plus one always equaled two and could never be three or four. He had certainly never considered that on the inner side of life, one plus one didn't always make two. Back in those days, his mother listened silently with a look of resignation on her face as Suguro's father spelled out the principles that guided his life.

It was early August when his father's younger brother arrived in Dalian. Suguro went to the harbor with his parents to welcome him. His uncle, dressed in his school uniform and carrying a tattered trunk in one hand, smiled broadly, showing his white teeth as he came down the landing bridge. He waved his free hand, shouting "Brother!"

As they rode in the horse-drawn carriage from the harbor to their home, Suguro's uncle peered left and right in wonder, asking his brother all sorts of questions, but Suguro's father sat with his arms folded, a disgruntled look on his face, while his mother answered as mediator.

Suguro did not particularly enjoy the three weeks his uncle stayed with them. While his father was off working for the Manchurian Railway, his uncle supervised Suguro's homework, and when he got stuck on an arithmetic problem or the reading of a kanji, with a scary face his uncle would poke his cheek with the pointed end of a pencil. Still, Suguro didn't dislike this uncle. When he finished his homework, his uncle, flashing that toothy smile, stripped down to his undershirt and played catch with him.

What was depressing for him were those nights when his father and uncle would get into arguments as they sat in the parlor. These disputes continued until late into the night, and Suguro was often awakened by his uncle's shouting voice.

"He is so infuriating!" His father would come out of the parlor with folded arms and complain to his wife, who was lying next to Suguro reading a book. "Just imagine my co-workers at the railway finding out that I have a brother with such dangerous ideas! They'd even start looking suspiciously at me."

His mother smiled and said, "You never worry about anyone except yourself."

Today, Suguro could imagine that the more his father disparaged his brother and tried to reform him, the more his mother took a liking to her brother-in-law. Suguro often observed his mother, who seldom uttered a word in her husband's presence, smiling at her brother-in-law as though she were his older sister and conversing cheerfully with him. Perhaps it had been his mother's secretive way of getting even with her husband.

When his uncle returned to Japan, Suguro's family once again went to the harbor to see him off. It was a rainy day, and the black ship carrying both cargo and passengers to Japan spilled sewage into the ocean while a line of coolies shouldering large bags of cement filed by those who had come to bid farewell to the passengers. Just before he boarded the ship, Suguro's uncle suddenly turned to his sister-in-law and said, "I may not ever see you again. But I intend to go on living by my convictions." Then, after firmly clenching Suguro's head, he grabbed his worn-out trunk with his right hand and climbed the gangway. A flock of gray seagulls flew back and forth, skimming the horizon and uttering their shrill cries; the ocean at Dalian harbor was somewhat rough. Her umbrella open, Suguro's mother watched the ship until it had almost disappeared into the distance.

That winter, Suguro's uncle gave the slip to the police who were tailing him and disappeared. He was never seen again. His family still had no idea where he had gone, or whether he had actually been murdered by the police. Whenever Suguro thought of this uncle, he remembered that white, toothy smile. And he recalled the image of his mother, staring after the ship as it disappeared on the horizon. What had his mother actually been looking at as she stood there holding her umbrella? The ocean? The ship heading out to sea? Or what lay ahead for her brother-in-law as he prepared to sacrifice himself in his own youthful way to the life he had chosen?

* * *

Suguro waited for Tatsu-san at a coffee shop. Tatsu-san, a country doctor, was a distant relative who had provided assistance to his mother when she was growing up in T Village. Tatsu-san had told him that he sometimes visited Tokyo since his daughter was living there with her husband. He had promised to meet Suguro the next time he came to Tokyo.

Tatsu-san came into the coffee shop wiping sweat from his face. He kept pulling a pocket watch from his wrinkled trousers, constantly worried about the time.

"I want to head back home on the 9:10 train."

"Well then, you still have two hours. I'll drive you to Tokyo Station. Have you had dinner?"

"Yeah, I did." He waved his hand as though irritated. Suguro sensed that from the moment he sat down in the booth, the old man really didn't want to talk with him. So for a time Suguro said nothing, merely puffing on his cigarette. But since his mother had no other living relatives, Tatsu-san was the only person he could get information from.

"I suppose it's not right of me to say this, but your mom, Setsu-san . . ." Tatsu-san said with a scowl, "I don't think she was really cut out to be a good wife."

A trickle of blood seeped from Suguro's heart, as though the blade of a knife had grazed his skin. He couldn't bear anyone other than himself criticizing or insulting his mother. Restraining himself as his face tensed up, Suguro finally managed a feeble smile.

"You can't have a hen crowing the hour, you know. Nothing good can come of a woman thinking about things other than housework and sewing." Tatsu-san spoke those last words as though he was spitting bitter medicine from his mouth.

The old man refused Suguro's offer to accompany him to Tokyo Station, instead waving down and climbing into a taxi with its "Vacant" sign illuminated. It was obvious from the way he scrambled into the taxi that he wanted nothing further to do with Suguro.

Unpleasant feelings after talking with Tatsu-san lingered in his chest after Suguro returned home. Still frustrated, he was changing out of his Western-style clothing when his wife suddenly said, "I have a favor to ask."

"What is it?"

"Do you think it would be all right if I went to an embroidery class a couple of times a week?—It would just be for about two hours each time. I got invited today."

A few times Suguro had heard from his wife that a group of housewives in the neighborhood got together to do heaven knows what. One of the group members had asked a teacher to instruct them in embroidery, and she had invited Suguro's wife to join them.

"As often as twice a week? And who will look after Minoru while you're gone?" Suguro scowled and puffed on his cigarette. When he refused to give her a definite answer, his wife stared at his profile and heaved a deep sigh.

* * *

Another autumn came to Dalian, followed by a long, dreary winter. Day after day new snow piled atop frozen layers of ice, while the smoke from the *pechka* ovens stained the snow black.

One day at school, Suguro's teacher unexpectedly called him out into the hallway.

"There's a message from your family. Your mother's been taken to the hospital. You need to go home right now."

Shouldering his backpack, Suguro walked out into the schoolyard where hard snow had piled up. Through the windows of the school building he could hear the voices of his classmates as they sat through another lesson. The sky was overcast again today, but as he passed through the school gate that was framed by poplar trees, his feelings of joy at getting out of school early outweighed his anxiety over the news that his mother had been hospitalized.

His mother had been admitted to the same hospital where he had previously been treated for an illness. But this time, the nurses he recognized who had been so kind to him now merely pointed to her ward sickroom with grim faces.

Suddenly a fear that his mother's condition might be critical churned in his breast.

He quietly pushed open the door with a "No Visitors" sign pasted to it. His aunt and father were standing beside his mother's bed, and a doctor was intently pointing a flashlight into her eyes.

"What's wrong with her? What's wrong with her?" Suguro asked his father, who stood with folded arms but gave no reply, so his aunt interceded and said in an unnaturally cheery voice, "Oh, she's just got a stomach ache. She'll be fine soon."

Timidly, Suguro looked from behind his aunt's back at his mother's sleeping face. She was snoring loudly as she slept. A rubber tube wet with saliva protruded from her mouth. A doctor was explaining something to his father and aunt, but all that Suguro could understand was that everything in her stomach had come out.

"Idiot!" his father muttered with folded arms after the doctor left the room. "The idiot!"

"You have to consider it an accident . . . We've got to tough this out for the time being," his aunt kept repeating to her brother. Listening to her, Suguro had a vague idea why his mother had been admitted to the hospital. Sitting in a chair, his legs trembled almost imperceptibly.

His mother was released from the hospital five days later. Every night thereafter, the lights shone from the parlor. It was the same parlor where his uncle and his father had constantly argued six months earlier. From time to time, he could hear his father's harsh voice and his mother's sobs. (Whenever he recalled the days of his youth, Suguro couldn't help but feel that everything surrounding him had been painted over with dark colors. He had painful memories of himself as he tried to avoid hearing his parents's voices by stuffing his fingers in his ears and lying motionless in his futon.)

He truly hated coming home after school. He hated seeing his mother lost in absent thoughts. Suguro would often head off in a direction opposite from that of his house, his satchel slapping against his back. An aged Russian man selling Russian bread sometimes followed him, his boots tromping on the frozen snow. In addition to bread, the old man, who had mucus caked in the corners of his eyes, also sold Christian medallions and hymnbooks. From time to time the old man would call out from behind Suguro, "Boy, where are you going?"

* * *

A fierce rain was falling. The rain hammered away for hours, its clatter like a ferocious pelting on stones, surging like a waterfall from the roof of Suguro's house and striking the *aralia* bushes in his garden. The torrential rain continued to fall throughout the morning.

The sun finally appeared in the afternoon. The drenched trees and the roof of his neighbor's house sparkled with a blinding light, and a blue sky quickly opened up; it was as though all of nature had come back to life and started to breathe again. Standing on the veranda, Suguro felt an emotion that might have been either remorse or self-reproach suddenly well up in his breast. He couldn't understand why he had unexpectedly been seized by such feelings, but somewhere inside his head, it was as though he could hear a voice saying, "Your life has all been a lie."

A short time later, he said to his wife, "Listen, don't you think we should start our lives all over again?" He had barely finished speaking before he began to wonder whether his question had been triggered by a fleeting excitement—the result of seeing the landscape restored to life after the rain, seemingly flushed with a vital life force.

"What would we start over again?"

"I'm not sure, but it feels like my life right now is misleading me."

"What are you talking about? Don't be ridiculous. After everything we've done so that we don't have to worry about the future." His wife looked over her shoulder at him as though he was mocking her. "You talk like a child."

He felt his momentary excitement drooping and fading away. He heaved a deep sigh and laid back on the tatami. Then he shook his head and said, "I'm going for a walk. Minoru, let's take a walk."

* * *

Suguro couldn't bear his father's invitations to accompany him on walks. And so, feeling anxious, he thrust both hands into the pockets of his soiled overcoat and slowly walked behind his father. The black, dirty snow that was still unmelted had been shoveled into heaps on both sides of the road, leaving only a narrow walkway in between that had been trampled hard by the soles of many shoes.

"You said you'd like a copy of *Jungle Book,* didn't you?" his father looked back at him and abruptly asked. "Hasn't your mother bought it for you yet?"

"Nope."

"Well, then, I'll buy it for you right now."

Jabbing at the hardly compacted snow with the tips of his boots, Suguro shook his head but said nothing.

"What's up? Don't you want it?"

"I borrowed it from a friend and read it."

But that was a lie. He wasn't sure why, but he hated to be sucked into the kindness expressed in his father's offer to buy him a book.

His father stared at his son with a disappointed look. "All right, listen carefully." His voice was suddenly harsh. "You may have already noticed, but . . ."

A tiny clump of snow crumbled under Suguro's boot.

"Your father isn't getting along very well with your mother. So we've decided we're going to live separately."

Gritting his teeth, Suguro crushed the broken clump of snow into a powder. Tears were welling up against his eyelids, but he kept telling himself, *You can't cry! You can't cry!*

"So you have to decide whether you'll live with your father or with your mother. Do you understand? Your mother is going to have to find a job now. It'll be hard for her to feed you and send you to school. Your mother says she'll do whatever is necessary to keep you with her, but . . ." His father paused. "Suppose you won't be able to keep going to school. If a person can't advance in school, he'll never be able to succeed when he goes out into society. So I think it would be best for you and me to live together. . . . Of course you'll be free to visit your mother."

Suguro didn't listen to anything else his father said. Standing in the middle of the deserted gray, snowy road, his father continued tediously jabbering to his son. His head full of confusion, Suguro stared vacantly at his father's moving lips.

"Is something wrong?"

"I hate this! I just hate this!" That was the best objection he could make to what his father was saying. It was obvious to him even as a child that his father was being unfair. He couldn't explain in words why he felt that way; all he knew was that his father was being unfair.

"I don't want to progress in school."

"Don't talk nonsense! If a man doesn't have a good education . . ."

How many times over the ensuing twenty or so years had that scene from his youth resurfaced in his heart? Whenever it did, tears would involuntarily fill Suguro's eyes. Thanks to that memory, the tears that he had held back on that twilight evening by gritting his teeth had repeatedly streamed down his cheeks after he became an adult. He wept not only because his father had been able to keep Suguro with him, using the flimsy reasoning that his son had to keep advancing through school. He suffered because of his own weakness and cowardice in forsaking his mother when he should have stayed with her even if it meant he couldn't keep going to school.

That night, Suguro's uncle and aunt came to his house and sat Suguro down with them.

"Listen, you'll be able to visit your mother whenever you want to. You're the heir to this house, so you've got to live here."

He said nothing in response to this pressure. His uncle and aunt concluded that his silence meant assent.

"You're a child. You don't have to worry about anything," his aunt said. "Leave everything to us."

* * *

Why at that time hadn't he been able to summon the courage to say "I'm going to live with my mother"? Had he been selfishly concerned about his own future? That may have been part of it. Had he been driven by concerns that he didn't know what sort of life he would have with his mother? Yes, that too. He wasn't without compassion for his father. There was no question that he felt utterly helpless as his aunt sweet-talked him. Many different factors were entangled together, leaving Suguro incapable of pointing to just one as the decisive motivation.

But whatever the reasons might have been, it did not change the fact that he had betrayed and abandoned his mother. Up until the present day, that fact had left a hard knot in the depths of his heart. The more he was driven by self-reproach, the more hateful his father became to him. Partly to gloss over his own weakness, he had distanced himself from his father. Even though he understood logically that he was acting irrationally, he could do nothing to change his feelings.

He still remembered that the morning after his uncle and aunt had coaxed him into living with his father, he had been unable to look his mother directly in the face. He had been trying not to make a sound as he ate the breakfast that their Manchu maid served him when his mother came into the parlor, her face swollen from weeping.

"Young man, you've dropped rice on the floor again," the maid said.

His mother sat down directly opposite him, and in a voice as calm as she could muster, she said, "Good morning. You're going to be late for school if you dawdle."

Suguro averted his eyes and flung down his chopsticks as he fled the parlor. Pursued by the painful awareness that he was a miserable, filthy coward for abandoning his mother, he put on his backpack. The words "Mother, I will live with you" had welled up in his throat like a sob, but when he started back to the parlor, he could hear his uncle and aunt talking.

"Setsu, you're already up?" His uncle spoke to Suguro's mother in an affected voice. "Is the morning paper here yet?"

Hearing that voice, Suguro despite himself stopped in his tracks. The words he had been about to say to his mother were left unspoken.

"You don't need to worry." His aunt had tiptoed up behind him as he was quietly pulling on his boots. "Your mother isn't angry with you. And nothing at all has changed, since you'll be able to see your mother any time you want. Although it turns out that she's going to be away from Dalian for about a month."

Suguro's aunt explained that his mother would be going on a trip for about a month and would return directly to Dalian. But that was nothing more than a ruse by adults who were trying not to upset a child any further. Foolishly enough, Suguro believed her. His mother, after all, had clearly promised him that she would be back in a month.

"You stay here and look after the place. And do everything your aunt tells you to do."

How painful the theatrics his mother had to perform for him must have been. Today Suguro was painfully aware of that. Had he been put in the same position, he would certainly have put on a similar show for Minoru. One morning about a week later when he woke up, his mother was gone. Nor was his father there. Nor were his uncle and aunt.

"If they were going to see her off, I wanted to go, too!" he lashed out at the Manchu maid through his tears. "Why didn't you wake me up?"

"The ship, it left so early. You would not be able to get up." The maid shook her head. "The ship, it left so early. You would not be able to get up."

* * *

A tiny whirlwind was swirling around the schoolyard. A sheet of newsprint spun into the air, flying off into the leaden sky. With one hand thrust into his pocket, Suguro watched as the newsprint floated away.

A middle-aged woman came out the entrance and slowly approached him on the deserted schoolyard.

"My name is Ayukawa, and you would be—?"

Suguro hurriedly bowed and explained that he was the son of Suguro Setsuko, who had worked here many years before. The woman gave a mild gasp of surprise and responded that she had been one of his mother's students.

"I heard that she passed away . . . I still haven't visited her grave to pay my respects." Looking at her wristwatch, she said apologetically, "I only had a class with her . . . I didn't know her very well."

But Suguro had in fact come here because he had found the name and address of this woman named Ayukawa in the little pocket diary he had found among his mother's belongings.

"My mother . . . she wasn't very popular among the students, was she?"

"Oh no, that's certainly not the case. Not at all," the woman hurriedly shook her head. "But she was a bit strict."

"In the way she taught?"

"That's right." She began to watch her words carefully. "Sometimes I think we students must have been quite slow and just couldn't keep up with her."

The whirlwind picked up another piece of trash and spun it into the air. Miss Ayukawa glanced at her wristwatch.

"What does that mean? I'm sorry, but I want to hear everything I can about my mother."

"I'm not quite sure how to put it, it's just that she was seeking something in music far beyond our imaginations, so those who couldn't keep up with her . . ." Miss Ayukawa's lips contracted into an ambiguous smile.

"What about those who couldn't keep up with her?"

"I suppose in various ways, she couldn't understand them."

The ambiguous smile still hovered on her lips. That smile seemed to him to be saying, "To be truthful, she was just more than we could handle." Just as Suguro's father had been at a loss how to deal with her, had her students also not known how to cope with his mother?

"I'm terribly sorry, but I have to . . ."

"No, I'm sorry to have taken up your time." Suguro hurriedly bowed his head.

Miss Ayukawa walked back slowly, just as she had come, across the deserted schoolyard and into the school building. Suguro, both hands in his pockets, stared at the school where his mother had taught music for three years after they left

Dalian. Like the elementary school she had attended, this school building had been completely rebuilt with concrete.

Those who couldn't keep up with her . . .

He could still hear Miss Ayukawa's voice. During the years of her marriage, his mother's smiles had always been meek but icy, perhaps because of the contempt she felt for Suguro's father, but after the divorce she developed an increasingly hot temper. At times she even became hysterical. He didn't want to remember those times. But he had to recall them in order to follow the trail of his mother's life.

Those who couldn't keep up with her . . .

He tried to picture how his mother must have looked when she was fired at this school. The principal had probably told her that music was taught at this school as part of the students's cultural education and that it was not a place to train future musicians. But to her mind, there was no such thing as teaching music as part of cultural education. Suguro could picture his mother's fingers, as stiff as crushed leather, pressing on the strings of her violin. In winter, her fingers were sliced by the strings and blood oozed out.

* * *

Suguro's father returned to Japan, taking his son with him, the year after his mother had come back to Japan. He had resigned his job at Southern Manchurian Railways and taken a position in the Hyōgo Prefecture Office of Education. By that time, Suguro was already in middle school.

Every single view of the Japan that he was seeing for the first time seemed filthy and small to him. The cities, the streets, the houses—all were beggarly and shoddy compared to those in Dalian. Across the road from Suguro's house, which was close to the Rokkō Station on the Hankyū train line, was an empty lot with a "For Sale" sign, and Suguro played there every day with other middle schoolers around his same age. But somehow he couldn't make himself fit in with them.

He knew of course that his mother was living in Tokyo. Letters from her came with great regularity, and his father had not tried to stop Suguro from replying to them. But neither did he make any effort to send Suguro to Tokyo to see his mother, nor did he send for her to come to Kobe. His mother never failed to write in her letters that she would someday bring Suguro to live with her. Suguro on the one hand hoped for such a day, but on the other feared that it might happen.

In September, his aunt visited Kobe from Dalian. She stayed in Suguro's house, but she almost never mentioned his mother in his father's presence. But one day she quietly summoned Suguro into the hallway.

"I'm sure you'd like to see your mother . . . ," she said in a whisper. "You don't need to worry. Sometime I'll make sure you get to see her. Just leave everything to me." But Suguro sensed in her words a cunning attempt at duplicity, and he kept his eyes on the floor and gave no response. And in the middle of that night as he was walking down the hallway to use the bathroom, he overheard through the sliding door his father talking with his aunt in the dimly lit parlor.

"Setsu doesn't seem to be getting along well no matter what she tries to do. I got a letter from Iguchi-san in Tokyo saying she had already changed jobs twice."

"She's the sort of woman who has no idea how to meet other people halfway," his father spat out the words. "It'll end up the same no matter where she goes."

"She really has to have a change of heart. The way she is right now, nobody is going to like her."

Standing in the hallway, Suguro recalled his aunt's wily face earlier that day when she had said "Just leave everything to me." He didn't know any of the circumstances, but he did understand that his mother had left one school position after another. Although she had written to him that she would someday bring Suguro to live with her, he felt he would be a burden to her if he went. Ultimately, just as his mother had failed in her married life, she would also never be satisfied with her employment.

That year, however, he was finally able to see her. She made the trip from Tokyo to Osaka. This mother he had not seen in such a long while seemed totally worn down, her face sallow. She wept when she saw him. They had lunch at a department store at Umeda, then went up onto the roof of the store and sat together on a bench. It was for him a day of happiness the likes of which he had not experienced in a long while.

"It doesn't matter what it is," she said to him. "I hope you can find something that no one but you can do. If it's something that anybody can do, then someone else will do it. Please think of something that you can do yourself."

"But father always says that the greatest happiness comes from being ordinary."

A bitter look crossed her face. "Give some careful thought to the reason your mother has worked so hard to live the kind of life she has."

* * *

As the words he had calmly listened to revived thoughts of his mother again and again in his heart, somehow they seemed to crystallize into a single word. But that happened many years later.

When he returned after school, he felt no love in his home without his mother there. Once his classes finished for the day, he went home only because he had nowhere else to go. His father's house, watched over by the maid. The afternoon snacks, provided merely out of duty. As he ate the snacks, he lay down, staring at the ceiling for a long time. He did no studying, nor did he even play. The sun was setting and the sliding glass doors clattered. His grades at school visibly plummeted, and his teachers concluded that he was past hope. His only merit lay in the fact that, while he didn't stand out at school, neither was he up to any mischief. But it wasn't that Suguro just didn't do anything mischievous; he was simply incapable of it.

His mother knew nothing of what was happening with Suguro. In her letters, sent three times a month, she wrote about things that were well beyond his capabilities. She encouraged him, for instance, once he graduated from middle school, to be sure to apply to a national university, or she insisted that his grades place him in the top ten students of his class. In reality, his grades put him third from the bottom. His teachers would have burst into laughter if he had told them he was going to apply to a national university. His mother knew none of this. Because he made sure to not write anything in his letters to her that would cause her disappointment. Since his father never sent a single letter to his mother, there was no possibility that his lies would be exposed.

Why did I lie to my mother back then?

It wasn't simple vanity that led him to tell lies that would surely be revealed at some point. It was his diffidence that caused him to avoid hurting his mother who was living by herself a long distance away. Not wanting to cause her any concern, Suguro ended up writing in his letters that he was in good spirits as he attended school each day.

At the end of that year, his aunt paid another visit to Kobe from Dalian. She was making arrangements for her family to move back to Japan, and she had also set up Suguro's father to meet a potential marriage partner.

"Come, sit down. Would you like me to cut you a slice of sweet bean jelly?" As she had often done in the past, his aunt lit a cigarette and had Suguro sit in front of her. "It must be lonely for you to have to come home after school and wait until your father returns, and we must remember that your father is a man, after all. I think he really needs a wife to take care of him."

Just as he had done when he was told of his mother's divorce, Suguro said nothing. His aunt took his silence as agreement.

"And out of consideration for your father and your new mother who'll be living here . . . you mustn't ever mention Setsu-san. No matter how much you're thinking about her on the inside, you mustn't ever say it out loud."

This was the first time that his aunt had ever called his mother "Setsu-san" in front of Suguro. And she had called the woman who would be marrying his father his "new mother." These expressions wounded Suguro deeply, but he said nothing. He didn't even tell his aunt he hated those words. He remained silent because he felt that he was on the verge of betraying his mother yet again. Initially the adults had said that Suguro was free to see his mother whenever he wished. But once he returned back to Japan, that was nearly impossible. And now, according to his aunt, a new woman would be his father's wife. Furthermore, he was told he must never talk about his mother in the presence of this woman and his father. Even though he hadn't been caught in a trap, he felt like an insect tangled up in a web. And no matter who was responsible, the fact remained that in effect he would be reduced to living a life in which he would forsake his mother and gradually leave her alone and abandoned.

"Listen. Nobody can survive in this world without experiencing this degree of pain," his aunt said, crushing her cigarette in the brazier. "You just have to endure it."

* * *

"Sorry you have to carry these," his stepmother said, a thin smile on her lips as she nimbly tied up the pickled daikon radishes in a wrapping cloth. "They aren't for you. I'm going to feed them to Chikako-san and Minoru."

"Good idea! You should take them with you," his father, in high spirits, said at the doorway. "But they smell really awful. Be careful with them." Then, treating it with great care, he picked up another package—this one containing his biography of Li Shangyin—and said, "Thank you for doing this."

Carrying the parcels in both hands, Suguro walked to the train station along the street lit by the setting sun. Both parcels were heavy and bothersome. He would have been hesitant to deliver even a novel he had written himself to a publisher, but how exactly was he supposed to take his father's manuscript, the contents of which he knew nothing, to Akebono Publishers? The package of pickled daikon that he had set on the bench at the station filled the air with a peculiar odor as he waited, his legs fidgeting, for the train to arrive.

The fact that I can't say no is a character flaw. Why didn't I just tell my father I wouldn't do it when he first brought it up?

Had he felt sorry there wasn't anything he could do to find a publisher for a manuscript that his father had worked so hard to produce? Seeing the eager look on his father's face, he had involuntarily been gripped by feelings of pity. Years earlier, he had ended up unable to say no to his aunt regarding his mother. Out of timidity he couldn't say no. That flaw in his character had left his mother feeling even lonelier than before. Gazing beyond the station at the clouds at sunset, Suguro once again tasted a mixture of remorse and self-reproach.

When he returned home, a motorcycle was parked in front of the entrance, and he got the feeling that something was amiss. He hurriedly opened the front door just as the local doctor was getting ready to leave. "Dear," his wife said quickly. "Minoru has a terrible fever."

"What happened?"

"Well, there is some reason for concern," the doctor said as he put on his shoes. "I was just talking to your wife about admitting him to the hospital."

"The doctor says in the worst case it might turn into polio."

"No, no," the doctor, seeing Suguro's face stiffen, waved his hand. "No, all I said was that if by any chance it might be polio, it was a good idea to play it safe. I really think it's just a cold."

His son slept listlessly, sweat dotting his forehead. Still in his suit, Suguro wrung out a washcloth in the basin at his bedside and wiped his burning forehead.

"Let's get him hospitalized."

"Do you think so? That probably is the safest."

After conversing in soft voices at the doorway with Suguro's wife, the doctor left.

"What do you want to do?"

"Me want to do? You've already decided, haven't you?" Suguro was almost shouting. "We'll hospitalize him."

"Can we afford it? What do you think?"

"I'll work it out somehow."

At a time like this, it would have been better not to have spent that twenty thousand yen, he thought, but it was too late. But twenty thousand yen wouldn't be enough to pay for hospitalization anyway.

* * *

"Yesterday, I went to Saga-san's music recital. As you know, I can't go to concerts that often these days (due to my financial situation), but Saga-san is a friend I've had since the time I studied with Mogilevsky, so I really wanted to go and listen to her. I hadn't seen her for eight years, but that's all the more reason I wanted to listen to her. To tell the truth, though, as her performance continued, I felt terribly disappointed. She played César Franck's Violin Sonata (You need to listen to it sometime), but her playing didn't rise above mere technique.

"For a long while I have struggled, living all by myself, and I haven't been able to look after you, either, but to make up for that, I have studied very hard. Every single day I put everything into my studies. So judging from my own studies, I felt that Saga-san's performance on the violin was merely technical, and that she doesn't know anything about what music really is. If technique were all there was to it, anybody could become skillful if they practiced, but I've always thought that there was something higher, much, much higher in music. When the concert was over and I was walking alone on the street at night, I thought about you. And I thought how much I wanted you not to become the kind of person who lives his life with nothing more than technique. Even if those around you urge you to take the easy way."

When he got home from school, that letter had been placed conspicuously on his desk. It was obvious that his stepmother was the one who had put it there. What had she been feeling as she plucked this letter out of the stack of mail and laid it on his desk? Suguro glanced quickly at the silent hallway before he opened the envelope. The tone of this letter was the same as all his mother's letters. They depressed and worried him. His mother expected too much of him. She demanded that he live the same kind of life she had. At some point, her demands became a burden for him, all the more so because they were underpinned by love. There was no denying that his mother's blood coursed through his body, but at the same time it was mixed together with the character traits he had inherited from his father. However much he might rebel against those traits, he had also acquired the tendency to try to live his life in tranquility, devoid of incident.

"Maybe I wasn't able to give you anything else, but unlike other mothers, I'm able to share with you the kind of life I have lived—at least, that's what I keep telling myself, feeling it's a kind of apology to you. An asphalt-paved road is safe, so anyone can walk along it. There's no danger, so anybody can walk along it. But if a person on that path turns and looks behind them, not a single one of their footsteps has been left on that safe road. A sandy beach by the ocean is difficult to walk along. It's a difficult path, but when you look behind you, every single one of your footsteps remains there. That's the kind of life your mother has chosen. Please, whatever you do, don't live a worthless life by walking on an asphalt road. Lately I seem to be having problems with my heart, and it worries me because sometimes I feel like my chest is suddenly tightening up."

The anxiety that welled up in Suguro's mind as he read this letter had less to do with his mother's heart and more to do with her oft-repeated injunction to avoid walking on the asphalt road. He hid the letter in his desk drawer out of concern for the problems it would cause him if his stepmother came across it while she was cleaning his room. He didn't want anyone—but especially his father, his aunt, and his stepmother, touching the letters from his mother. Still, the secretive content of this letter weighed as heavily on his heart as had all her previous ones.

He lay back on the tatami and stared at stains on the ceiling until darkness set in. He had no desire to study, despite what she had said in her letter. It came from a desire to take just a bit of revenge on his father, but also because he didn't want to please his father by improving his grades. His stepmother came into his room without saying a word, glancing at him lying on the floor. She silently put the socks and underwear she had washed for Suguro into his chest of drawers and left the room. It was obvious from her retreating figure that she had hurriedly taken care of his laundry from nothing more than a sense of duty.

"You've asked me when I might put on a concert, but right now I don't feel at all like doing one. I don't yet have any pieces that I could perform for others. Although there is surely something much higher in music than just technique, I still haven't grasped it, no matter how hard I practice. But I want to catch hold of something in one single note that surpasses just its sound. Lately, though, my heart has gotten worse, and everyone says how badly my face has swollen up."

* * *

On the night of moon-viewing in mid-autumn, Suguro's stepmother set out a vase filled with pampas grass and a tray stacked with rice dumplings. After dinner, his father, who had finished bathing, put on his summer yukata robe and sat down on the veranda, using a fan to cool himself.

"What a beautiful moon! Come look!" He drank his beer with relish and invited his wife to have a glass, too. "Here we are, all together as a family, gazing at the moon. It's wonderful." In fine spirits, he glanced at Suguro and his second wife. "Another uneventful year, nobody gossiping about us behind our backs . . . This is what real happiness means."

"Another of Papa's moral discourses," Suguro's stepmother said as she offered him a dumpling. "I'm tired of hearing them."

"Doesn't matter if you're tired of them. I'm just saying what's true."

The moonlight shone white on their tiny garden and on the empty lot beyond it. From time to time a train on the Hankyū line rattled by. Suguro gazed at his father's self-satisfied profile as the old man sat with a plate balanced on his lap. His temples throbbed as he ate a dumpling. His stepmother's temples throbbed, too. As he studied their profiles,

Suguro wondered to himself how these two individuals felt deep inside about Suguro's mother. Had they forgotten all about the fact that there was a lonely woman hidden behind the unperturbed happiness in which his father basked? Suguro, his head lowered, held tightly to the plate in his hand, overcome by a muffled anger toward his father and stepmother.

"Is something wrong? Why aren't you eating?"

"Oh, my! You usually eat five or six of them."

All Suguro's could do was to give his stepmother a feeble smile. He felt an unbearable disgust at himself for offering even that forced smile.

* * *

Suguro sat politely erect in the lobby of the Imperial Hotel. He was strangely embarrassed in such surroundings by the dust on his shoes and the threadbare knees of his pants and couldn't help being bothered by them. He felt as though the foreigners sitting nearby were staring disparagingly at him.

The heavyset Saga-san stopped in the center of the lobby, nodded after a busboy indicated where she could find Suguro, and briskly came toward him. She was considerably older than she appeared in newspaper or magazine photographs, and she seemed in poor health. Her makeup and clothes, selected to provide her a youthful appearance, had the opposite effect of making her wrinkles stand out.

"So you're Setsuko's son, are you," the woman said, her eyes wide as she studied Suguro's clothing. "I met you once before, in Dalian. Look at you now: you were so tiny then."

She took a cigarette and a small tin from her purse, and

as she placed a white pill in her mouth, she said, “You can hear me wheezing, can’t you? I have a bad heart.”

“My mother had a bad heart, too.”

“Yes, I know.”

She lit her cigarette. Suguro recalled that when this woman had stayed at his family’s home in Dalian many years before, the burning tip of her cigarette flickered red in the dark. Saga-san had reproached Suguro’s mother for giving up on the violin.

“She was an unlucky woman, Setsuko was.”

Her comment stung Suguro. From his father’s perspective, Suguro’s mother had not even been able to handle married life. But Suguro could say nothing in response to this assertion that his mother was unlucky when Saga-san herself was a violinist. His mother had not performed a single concert after returning to Japan. Or better perhaps to say that she was unable to perform a concert. Was there anywhere in this world someone who would sponsor a violin concert by an unremarkable music teacher?

“What it came down to was that Setsu-san . . .” Saga-san popped another pill into her mouth, “. . . She held too tightly to the reins.”

“The reins?”

“Yes, she would never let up on the reins. When you’re dealing with someone like that . . .”

Saga-san didn’t finish her sentence. But Suguro could tell from her tone how she felt about his mother. Saga-san’s fingers holding her cigarette. Those fingers were not as worn down as his mother’s had been. They had not been ripped open by the violin strings and discolored like cracked leather.

It was raining after he thanked Saga-san for her time and

left the hotel. As he walked in the soaking rain, a fierce anger shot up inside him. His father could say whatever he wanted about his mother. His father was an uncultured boor. And his aunt was free to think whatever she wished about his mother. His aunt knew nothing about truly living. But he could not bear to have either his mother's pupil, Ayukawa-san, or Saga-san, her friend from her days at the music school, speak disparagingly now about the way his mother lived her life.

"I'm seeking something much higher than simply music," his mother had frequently written in her letters to him. That woman searching for "something higher" was his own mother, and this was how she was viewed by society. *There's no way you people can understand my mother's way of life. You don't understand it, but as her son, I do,* he kept muttering to himself.

Still, by the time he returned home his agitation had subsided to a degree. His wife's younger brother, bored with looking after their house, called out when Suguro opened the front door, "You're back. My sister has gone to the hospital to see Minoru."

When Minoru was hospitalized two days earlier, the doctors had ruled out the possibility that he had contracted polio, but since he was prone to asthma, once they determined that he had bronchitis, they decided to keep him at the hospital for four or five days to give him a chance to rest.

When his brother-in-law left, Suguro settled down to work. The translation he was working on that day was taking more time than he had anticipated, so even when his wife got home he had only been able to complete five or six pages. In the dimly lit kitchen his wife was noisily chopping something with a knife as she prepared dinner. Her sister, she reported, had relieved her at the hospital and was staying with Minoru.

He took his father's manuscript from its envelope and flipped through the pages. Suguro had no interest whatsoever in the Chinese poet Li Shangyin. Apparently his father had written about this poet he was fond of just so he'd have something to do. Suguro skipped through the pages and aimlessly skimmed over something that seemed to be an Afterword: "I've read this poet's works over the course of many years, whenever I was happy, or when I was sad. Each time, I found something that touched the strings of my heart."

With a half-smile on his face, Suguro placed the manuscript back into its envelope. Suddenly his father's words from years earlier flashed through his mind: "Literature is something that's okay as long as it's nothing more than a hobby." Suguro found it both amusing and foolish that a man like his father could write something so glib in an Afterword. Yet his father, now approaching old age safe and secure with his place in the world, had written this manuscript and entrusted it to his son in the hope of getting it published. (*Mother had never even been able to have her own concert.*) With anger welling up once again in his chest, he went to the kitchen to get a drink of water.

"Done with your work?" his wife asked. "There's something I want to talk to you about."

"What is it?"

"The charges for the hospital are a lot more than I thought they'd be. Including the cost for the scans, it's going to be around thirty thousand yen. How are you going to handle that?"

He didn't reply. He knew exactly what she was thinking when she said "How are you going to handle that?"

"Your kimonos," he grumbled. "Why don't you just sell them?"

"I don't think we have to go that far . . . Can't you borrow some money from your father?"

"Absolutely not," he shook his head. "I don't want to borrow anything from my father."

But Suguro knew he would wind up going to his father to borrow the thirty thousand yen. He had previously borrowed money from his father to pay for his wife's pregnancy and again when he was laid up at the end of the year with the flu.

"So if you don't want to borrow it from your father . . . Do you have some other place you could get the money?"

"Why do you think I'm telling you to sell your kimonos?"

He continued to doggedly insist until his wife began to cry. Through her tears, she cried, "What gives you the right to look down on your father?!"

"You know nothing about this . . . How dare you talk to me like that!"

"I'll talk that way if I want. You'll never be the man your father is!"

Suguro's hands were shaking, and without thinking he made a move as though he would strike her, but he could not do it. He lowered his eyes and thought of his mother's face in death. In a dark, one-room apartment, a potted rubber plant off in one corner, shadows of agony lingered on his mother's pale forehead.

Credits

These credits constitute a continuation of the copyright page.

The Japanese novella and stories that are translated in this volume first appeared in the publications listed below, all © Shūsaku Endō Estate. English translations © Yale University unless otherwise noted.

"Mothers" (Haha naru mono) originally appeared in the journal *Shinchō* (January 1969); reprinted in book form in *Nihon no bungaku, 72: Nakamura Shin'ichirō, Fukunaga Takehiko, Endō Shūsaku* (Chūō Kōronsha, 1969); subsequently included in the collection *Haha naru mono* (Shinchōsha, 1971). English translation © 1984 by Van C. Gessel, originally appeared in *Stained Glass Elegies,* copyright © 1959, 1965, 1969, 1973, 1979 by Shūsaku Endō. Reprinted by permission of New Directions Publishing Corp and Pushkin Press Ltd.

"A Six-Day Trip" (Muikakan no ryokō) originally appeared in the journal *Gunzō* (January 1968); reprinted in the collection *Kagebōshi* (Shinchōsha, 1968).

"Spring in Galilee" (Gariraya no haru) originally appeared in the journal *Gunzō* (October 1969); reprinted in the collection *Haha naru mono* (Shinchōsha, 1971).

"A Fairy Tale" (Dōwa) originally appeared in the journal *Gunzō* (January 1963); reprinted in the collection *Aika* (Kōdansha, 1965).

"Shadows" (Kagebōshi) originally appeared in the journal *Shinchō* (January 1968); reprinted in the collection *Kagebōshi* (Shinchōsha, 1968). English translation © 1993 by Van C. Gessel, originally appeared in *The Final Martyrs,* copyright © 1959, 1968, 1976, 1978, 1979, 1981, 1983, 1984, 1985 by Shūsaku Endō. Reprinted by permission of New Directions Publishing Corp and Pushkin Press Ltd.

"Confronting the Shadows" was originally published in *Kage ni taishite* (Shinchōsha, 2020).

SHŪSAKU ENDŌ (1923–1996) is one of the most important and far-reaching Japanese authors of the twentieth century, praised for his incisive explorations of the fraught relationships between Eastern and Western cultures and religions. He was born in Tokyo in 1923, and soon after his birth, his family moved to Dalian in Manchuria. At his mother's insistence, he was baptized a Catholic at the age of twelve. During his studies at the University of Lyon in France in the early 1950s, he contracted a case of pleurisy that plagued him throughout his life. Major novels by Endō include *Silence* (1966), *The Samurai* (1980), and *Deep River* (1993). Long considered a contender for the Nobel Prize in Literature until his death in 1996, he received many awards during his lifetime, including the Akutagawa Prize, the Noma Literary Prize, the Tanizaki Prize, and the Order of Culture, Japan's highest honor for its creative artists. He is the author of scores of full-length prose works, including fiction and nonfiction, and numerous short stories and essays. The Shūsaku Endō Literary Museum in Nagasaki is devoted to the writer's life and works.

VAN C. GESSEL is an emeritus professor of Japanese at Brigham Young University and previously served as a chair of his department and dean of BYU's College of Humanities. He earned his doctorate in Japanese literature at Columbia University and joined the BYU faculty in 1990. He previously taught at Columbia and the University of Notre Dame, and was on the faculty at the University of California, Berkeley, for eight years. He has translated nine of Endō's works into English; consulted for the film version of *Silence,* directed by Martin Scorsese, which was released in 2016; and in 2018 was inducted into the Order of the Rising Sun by the Japanese government.